Following Shepard

First Printing, 2016

ISBN 9780692667620

This book is dedicated to my parents, who are far better
than any of the ones inside it.

I also offer special thanks to Jennifer Dillard, Joshua Judkins,
and Scott Britton, whose insights helped ensure
that this is something other people would want to read.

Introduction

This book has been in the works for ten years. Its story mirrors my own journey in more than a few ways. At various times in my adult life I have identified with nearly every character to some degree. When I first started writing it, I believed that it would be an insight into the American gay rights movement. I believed that among gay audiences, it would speak some of the feelings we at times found hard to put into words. Among straight audiences, I hoped it would explain some of the anger and frustration we felt.

But as the writing began to take much longer than expected, the movement changed shape as well. I had largely set aside this book because I was no longer sure it was relevant to anyone save myself. But in the wake of June 26, 2015, the book has new meaning to me. We are no longer the radically oppressed minority we were. The generation that has grown up since that time is having a completely different experience. We are now the majority — and our rights have majority support.

It's important, then, to look back at this brief time in our roots. Just before the dawn of social media, and over the worst of AIDS, this pocket of our history shaped the conversations to come. I hope that this story has new relevance for us, and insight into the obstacles we faced, and some of the problematic way that we addressed them.

This book didn't set out to be historical fiction. But I am proud that it ended that way.

1

This is the room; Eirinn knows it instinctively. This motel bed is the one that held Seth the night before. It is our fourth night, and we are now one day behind.

Eirinn prepares the bed and undresses with practiced precision. He peels back the corner of the sheets at a careful angle, even though they wrinkle and shift with every move. The motel sheets and rough wool blanket fold off the corner to a crisp triangle. His slender frame is only bare a moment. As he surrounds the pillow with both hands and collapses immediately into sleep, I wonder what it must feel like to come to your lover's bed a day too late.

As Eirinn sleeps, I begin to organize my notes from the car ride today. It is less work than the day before.

After Christmas of last year, Eirinn Gallagher and Seth McCam went to Ireland by themselves. Gallagher characterizes the trip as "a terrible mistake. A series of terrible mistakes." Gallagher had been four times with his family. McCam had never left the continental US.

"For one thing," Gallagher said, "December is not the best time to travel to Ireland. It's not as cold as you think, that far North, but it is dark most of the time."

"Dark?"

"In the summer, the sun can set as late as 10 at night. But we pay for it in the winter. Nights are not especially cold compared to America, but they are very long. So Seth and I didn't get in much sightseeing."

Gallagher has no brogue or red hair, but his kinship to the isle is clear, even before knowing his surname.

"How long did you stay?"

"A week. We came back to classes three days late, just to get that."

"What did you do?"

"I visited my family; Seth slept a lot. His headaches were bad that first weekend. He had to go to the hospital one night."

"He went to the hospital for headaches?"

"Actually he blacked out from one. He tried to cover up, say that he was feeling better one night, and — well, it got the better of him and he blacked out on me. I panicked and took him to the hospital."

"They didn't do too many tests; I'm not sure they believed me that it wasn't the alcohol."

"You had been drinking."

"Yeah, but only a little. We hadn't had that much."

"Couldn't Seth have had some you weren't aware of?"

"I was pouring."

I can't extrapolate or imagine Eirinn's reaction in the moment of these events. In the car, with me, Eirinn was giving an indifferent confession. Whatever catharsis that came with this thing had already happened, or had yet to.

I never imagined big stories happened like this. It was always my understanding that even contrived stories were wrapped with emotion, that sensational headlines were born that way. But this was not calculated; his narrative was a summation of the events, point by point. He had been with Seth, now he was driving halfway across the country to find Seth again, and telling me the story of the inbetween.

———————————————

I stop the tape, and pull off my headphones. My hand is cramping.

Nearly everything around us is stained, brown and feels as though it was made before 1975. The floor to ceiling wood paneling clinches the motif. It is unlikely, even when the wainescotting was first installed, that it concealed the imperfections in the wall. Now, the warped lines in the plywood are a contour map to every water stain bulge in the room's thin walls.

The dresser is worn and battered in one corner. It looks as though someone paid lip-service to refinishing it several years ago. There are layers of carvings in it; initials, names, and random scratch marks laid in over time, and so it is hard to pick out the fresh pentagram, except that there is still sawdust in the engraving.

The loud heating unit beneath the window of the room grumbles to life. The machine's waking noise is full of clicks it shouldn't have, but hot air emerges nonetheless. A sliver of the darkness outside appears every minute or so. The rigid, polyester curtains wave in and out as one unit, having been starched into oblivion. I open them. Outside the glass is a boy our age, walking by with an ice bucket. It is startling to both of us, and I freeze while my heart pumps heavily. Though I did not see him approach, I imagine he continues quicker than he came until he reaches his room. I close the curtains again.

It is the adrenaline that reminds me how tired I am. My mind is fogged from lack of sleep, and no amount of caffeine will clear it. I cannot sleep, however. I start the tape and put my headphones back on.

———————————————

"So the hospital thought he had passed out from drinking?"

"Seth wasn't helping my argument. He was coming back from the second vision."

"The what?"

"In my bag, on the back seat. Pull out the black and white composition book."

3

Seth McCam kept three journals. Each book was an unwitting gift from the parents in his life. Twelve-year-old McCam dropped a composition book in the cart while shopping with his mother, and so purchased himself a book to record his dreams. At sixteen, seeing a gift from Dillon Gallagher unused on Eirinn's shelf, he had taken a hardcover blankbook to record his daily activities. And finally or firstly, as the date is unknown, he took an old, worn and leather-bound volume from his father, and began to write in it, as well.

The log of McCam's life is ordinary. Regular entries in consistent handwriting, all in the same pen kept clipped to the book. Entries are dated about three to a week; there is no mechanical regularity to their spacing. The last entry is mid-August before he entered college, but there's no indication that it was intended as a final entry.

The book of his dreams doesn't begin as unusual either. It is full of the anxieties and anxious fantasies one would expect the 12 – 18-year-old to have; having sex, losing his mother, being teased at school, etc. In the journal, Seth's ability to describe the dreams quickly grows in memory, vocabulary and style, while his handwriting does not. It is inconsistent, scratched down in a bleary rush with whatever was handy.

The final two entries in Seth's dream journal are called "VISIONS." The final entry, "SECOND VISION," is as follows.

> I am being buried alive. I am lying naked in the ground; the hole is shallow and being filled in with white snow and earth. The figure with the shovel is obscured, but I see wings on his back and a key at his belt. I can not speak, or scream. The figure continues to shovel. The key is bronze. It is oxidized and warped. Spots are blackened, and others covered in a fine white ash. This key is one of three. The shovel is old; blade rusted by soil and chipped by stone, smooth where hands have held it before, rough and dirt-covered everywhere else. But the figure's hands do not match. They are wrinkled, but not calloused or hardened. They are my father's hands. Now I see his face, clearly. It is dead. His eyes are sunken and purple and his face is smeared with dirt.
> Snow and earth falls on my face again and again, until the world turns dark.

"He was yelling about it when we brought him into the hospital. It didn't help my case much."

"I can imagine."

For the first time, Eirinn's face was stern. He did not look from the road, but written in profile was the weight of what had happened to him, and the fear playing underneath. He continued to drive.

"You should read more of the journals."

> June 6, 1996 – I remembered the time she took me out of school in third grade. It wasn't a whole memory, I don't think; lots of the day I don't remember. But I remember she showed up early in the morning in the classroom and called to me and I came, and the teacher asked what was going on and she said I wasn't feeling well. The teacher tried to have a talk with her outside of class, but she laughed and told me to come with her. I don't remember where we went that day, but I remember the look on the teacher's face and my mother's laugh. She used to take me out of class a lot like that, when she was between jobs.

I grab the journal again from the artifacts Eirinn brought. A picture stuffed in the book presents itself when I turn the page, not having been pasted but instead seemingly stuffed in, whether as a bookmark or hiding place is unclear. Eirinn is the center but not the focus of the photo, asleep next to Seth, who is smiling obnoxiously and holding the camera at arm's length. Seth's smile is wide and an unusual shape, uneven and captivating. Much the same way as eyes directed at a lens will follow the viewer, Seth's smile seems pointed in a single direction, at me.

Both boys are also apparently naked in the photo, Eirinn presumably without his knowledge.

The relationship between Eirinn Gallagher and Seth McCam is unusual in many ways. The boys share a bed, nightly. Far more unusual is the fact that the boys have never, as Eirinn puts it, successfully had sex with each other.

I do not know why his frankness in that conversation was so unnerving.

5

They are the kind of best friends who do not remember the first time they met, it was so far in their infancy. As a very young child, Eirinn spent many afternoons and evenings at Seth's house; his parents working late in direct contrast with the McCams, Matthew always arriving shortly after the end of school, and Katelyn often home all day anyway. Eirinn remembers enjoying most the times when both Seth's parents were home, and with each other; it was often the only time he had alone with Seth, not under his father's watchful eye or his mother's constant intercession into play.

Seth did not come to the Gallagher household, except on Eirinn's birthday. It wasn't a rule, at least not a written one, but whenever Eirinn would invite Seth, there would be an excuse not to come, or not to get together at all. Over the years, Eirinn never questioned it.

In the far bed, Eirinn looks precisely the same as the picture, at least until his mouth starts to hang open and he drools more than a little. I lose the pages the photo was stuck between, and decide if I'm going to remember any of this or function in the morning, sleep is going to be required.

2

Eirinn picks up the diner menu out of habit, and looks it over out of curiosity, but he made his decision before walking in the door. When I take a minute for my own decision, Eirinn isn't impatient with me. It's surprising: this diner breakfast is the first time we've consumed food at less than 50 miles an hour since we first got in the car. Our trip has been punctuated by foot tapping stops at convenience stores, and Eirinn's impressive ability to be quietly impatient with the speed of fast food. This morning is not that.

The diner is next to the motel where we stayed, but there's little else at the exit. A few pickup trucks are parked outside, and three semis behind the motel. The whole exit is a poorly aged anachronism. Both the diner and motel were built at a time dominated by chains and franchises. But the signs: "motel" and "diner" are a pretty clear indicator of private ownership. Even if they weren't, the haphazard color scheme is pretty telling. The diner's exterior is wooden siding, stained inconsistently across the building. The diner, meanwhile, has touches of chrome, but is largely faded yellow on the exterior and dirty yellow on the interior. When they were first painted, I suspect they were the same color. The cliche chrome band circles the edge of the table in the booth. The vinyl in our booth is in good shape — the next one over has been patched by duct tape six times.

Outside the window are few passers-by, only two while we wait for the waitress to greet us. Through the glass, I can not shake the feeling that they are staring at us. But once inside, they greet the waitress with familiarity and don't give us a second glance.

The waitress, picking up on Eirinn's serene certainty and smile, looks at him first. "Pancakes."

She smiles back. It's genuine, and the first indication I've seen in almost a week that Seth isn't the only one with the infectious personality. My order is more mechanical, and expected.

"Two eggs over easy, toast and bacon. And tea."

The diner is not a big place. Sound travels well, but to my disappointment, the only lingo I hear between waitress and short order cook is "Ya' got that, Hal?" and a grunted assent from behind the serving window six feet away.

Eirinn closes his eyes and breathes in the warmth of the morning sun. Where we're sitting, it's on his face. His hair is unkempt and the sun catches the wild strands, lightening them to a beach blonde. He's elsewhere, in his mind, as he's been many times on the trip; but for once it seems to be a happy place.

"We had one good summer."

I'm learning, and though the story that's about to start was unexpected, I've got the tape ready this time.

"Seth's family always used to do summers on Lake Erie, where they rented a place in a little chatauqua. Matthew (Seth's father) taught classes up there, so admission was comped and rentals were cheap. I was never able to go, until Summer after Junior year. I stayed a week and we spent the whole time together."

"What's a chatauqua?"

"They mostly don't exist anymore. The concept is like an adult educational retreat. They used to have a focus on religious education, but the few remaining have become family vacation spots with a smattering of educational background."

He correctly reads my surprise and confusion.

"I only looked it up because Seth dropped it into casual conversation once like it's a word everybody knows."

"So what was this place like?"

"It's a gated community. There's admission to get in, and once you're there, they have a bunch of activities. It's — imagine somebody put the suburbs on hold 50 years ago."

"Oh. I guess that's not the best place to be gay."

"Well, I assume they're not judgmental. They're nice people, but the reason we wouldn't do anything public is that it's also small. The whole thing is less than a square mile and everybody knows everybody. We agreed Matthew shouldn't find out about us until we were financially independent. It makes things complicated. He couldn't see us together, but neither could anybody else who might bring the story back."

"So no public displays of affection at all."

"Or private, in any places Seth couldn't be absolutely certain anyone might enter. It wasn't like we could just rent a hotel room. You have to understand, if we were caught it was the end of Seth's future. We had no idea how Matthew would react but it wouldn't have been good. Disowning was on the table. We couldn't afford that risk."

Eirinn rubs his finger along a crack in the wooden table. He claims the decisions were made together, but he doesn't meet my eyes.

"So that left you with nowhere to go."

"Almost. Ever since he'd started coming up to Lake Erie, Seth had taken sailing lessons. Seth knew the guys so well he took a boat out whenever he wanted, and he took me with him. Every day we'd go out and lay together, just letting the waves carry us for hours. I'm pretty sure the sailing guys knew what was going on, but I never told Seth for fear he'd deny us even that."

"Even out there, you didn't do anything?"

"Sailing was always something Seth had done with Katelyn [Seth's mother]. It didn't exactly put him in the mood. Well, that and those boats are tiny."

"What about your parents?"

"I haven't told them."

"What do you think will happen when you do?"

The distant look disappears from his eyes, and he looks straight into mine. I wonder if the intensity is intentional from the start, as he looks away the moment contact is made.

"I don't know."

There's silence between us for another moment. It's one of several times over the past few days that the gravity of a question grew as it was answered.

It's clear that Eirinn has considered the possible outcomes of that conversation. He hasn't romanticized what it might turn out to be. I don't press the issue, but Eirinn seems to realize this is a rare opportunity to talk it through, even if it's to someone who will only understand half of it.

"Mom's a nurse, and Dad's a psychiatrist. And the medical community has said gay is normal for 30 years now. So it seems like I should be fine."

Eirinn takes a bite. The reversal that's happened in his mind a hundred times spills out.

"But I'm their only son. Their only child. It changes the math. I've seen it — change the math."

"But what about... isn't your family Catholic?"

Eirinn legitimately laughs. It's quiet and short but it returns the smile to his face.

"That's not a factor. We're... not Catholic like other people are."

The waitress brings my tea. The porcelain mug makes a familiar clink against the saucer. It's a pleasant sound to me — Eirinn seems suddenly struck with inspiration.

"Can I get some orange juice please?"

She clearly sees the same halo-framed smiling face I've been talking to for the past few minutes. She's been standing behind the counter, talking to regulars and having a routine day — but his smile makes it brighter.

"Absolutely, hon."

People wish they could love a food like Eirinn Gallagher loves pancakes. Our orders come, and he is quiet. By this point he's smiling in spite of himself. I'm hungry and more than ready to start eating, but the first bite he takes is a sight not to be missed. The sliver he cuts is perfectly shaped, lightly touched in syrup and delicately delivered to his mouth, where he melts instead of it. It suddenly seems absurd to me that I've ordered something other than pancakes.

As we leave, the waitress waves at us. She's still smiling.

3

Katelyn McCam died on April 24, 1996, just two months after she told her family that she had pancreatic cancer. She had known it herself for approximately a year and a half. She was 44. Matthew was 47. Seth was 16.

Eirinn Gallagher describes Katelyn as a selfish woman, but the facts don't seem to paint any conclusive picture, and everyone with anything to say on the subject seems to have a different story to tell.

She was born June 6, 1951, to a professor of English and a substitute high school teacher. The family moved a lot, about every four to five years throughout Katelyn's childhood. Katelyn herself never held down a single job for that long. Her resume is a long string of jobs with 2-years tenure and 6 month breaks in-between. Her longest job was her last one, where she was employed until she died.

Coworkers all remember a fiery, deeply funny woman. Aggressively competent, but never there for the long haul. In interview, several men speak of her nervously. Eirinn thinks these are the ones she slept with.

When he was 13, and she was 42, Eirinn was waiting at a bus stop when he saw her enter a motel with another man. He was younger, handsy, and obviously eager. His eyes were only focused on Katelyn. She looked to him with a playful smile, until she saw Eirinn across the street. She looked towards him, and their eyes met for a moment. Eirinn looked down to the pavement. It was cracked and gray and offered no respite or distraction from what he had seen. By the time he looked up again, they had entered the room and disappeared from sight. Eirinn had a wooden keychain at the time, a gift from Seth he'd owned for 7 years. It was rubbed smooth from worry and fidgeting. But his fingernail slipped at the sight of Katelyn and the motel, and left a scratch he never rubbed smooth. He got rid of the key chain a month later. Every look at the scratch brought him back to the moment when he knew his best friend's mother was cheating on his father.

Neither Katelyn nor Eirinn ever spoke of what they had seen to the other, and Eirinn knew better than to break the news to Seth. In elementary school, another boy had once claimed that his father was sleeping with Katelyn McCam. It was the only fight Seth had ever gotten into. The boy needed 20 stitches in various locations around his body. Biting was involved. Matthew had come to pick up his son, who staunchly refused to tell either of his parents what the fight had been about.

Katelyn donated an average of 14% of her income to charity each year, and was a primary investor in over 10 small businesses, one of which was Dillon Gallagher's fledgling psychiatry practice. Upon discovering she had pancreatic cancer, she made a large donation to the American Cancer Society and personally recruited over $60,000 in donations from friends and co-workers.

Katelyn's last job lasted three and a half years, and with it she earned enough to set up a trust fund for Seth's college. Even this she kept from her husband and son until the reading of her will. Eirinn insists that this is only further evidence of her selfishness and emotionally closed nature.

She was very close with her son, and used the many breaks between her jobs to take him places, sometimes far, and usually without Matthew. Sometimes they would fly across country, other times drive out for a day trip. Seth's excused absences were maxed out nearly every year of his schooling from the long weekends or even random weekdays that Katelyn would arrive to whisk him away.

Eirinn knew her longer than any other interview I am able to secure, but he does not claim to be an unbiased perspective. I believe it says something beyond my own frustration that nobody is able or willing to speak to the whole substance of her character. Coworkers didn't know her for longer than her tenure. She lost touch with every friend from college, and every friend before that. Without Matthew, without her parents (who died 10 years earlier) there is no one to tell the full story. My access to the McCam family files shows the paper trail, but a stack of tax returns and insurance forms are barely a keyhole into the life of a person.

Katelyn McCam made only one lifelong friend, and she married him, but cheated on him at least once. Amongst the many facts, and the loud voice in my ear, the one certain trait of Katelyn's that emerges out of the blanks. I don't know her favorite color. I don't know her worst fear. I don't know the proudest moment of her life. I know none of her lasting passions, shallow or deep. I don't know what dreams filled her sleep, or what nightmares disrupted them. It's not my ignorance of these facts and feelings that scares me; it is my belief that no one ever knew them. She didn't share the whole of herself with Matthew, or Seth; and no one else was in her life long enough to see more than a fraction of her.

This empty legacy, not the cancer or the unfocused career, the loss of her parents or the illicit affair, is the tragedy of Katelyn McCam, at least in my mind. All of us are forgotten after a generation or two — the bulk of what made up Katelyn McCam was forgotten in less than a decade after her death.

After he was told of his mother's cancer, arrangements were made for Seth to complete his school assignments from home. He didn't come to school, or go out at all; Eirinn didn't see Seth until the funeral. Seth didn't recount the event in his journal, but Eirinn remembers it very well.

The church was standing room only. Pew after pew was packed with people, most of whom had clearly never been in a cathedral before, and many wearing various forms of cancer awareness paraphernalia — ribbons, buttons, t-shirts — all of it seeming out of place to Eirinn. He sat with his family, who weren't even able to get a pew in the front half of the church, or see the remaining McCams. Most of the eulogies were about the awful truths of cancer — neither Seth nor his father got up to speak. Only one woman, an old college friend, seemed to speak to Katelyn's character, one Eirinn had never seen before, and never saw again.

"I didn't get to him until after the mass, at the receiving line. Seth and his dad were the only immediate family, so they rode in their own limo, sat in a reserved section of the church, and he didn't reach out to me to join him. I hadn't seen him in two months, until the receiving line after the funeral mass."

Eirinn describes Seth as pale and drained. People passed him by, some offering vague comfort, but he refused to shake hands or even look up at anyone. Seeing Seth was difficult. Grief was new to Eirinn. His ears hurt and his throat clenched and the world disappeared. This was pain, and he'd never even liked her.

But Eirinn swallowed, stepped up and removed Seth from the line. They went into a side room of the church, an old library with a couch gathering dust. They had hidden here together several times before when Matthew had volunteered for a reconciliation service.

The light was out; dim colors filtered in through the stained glass. It was in this room, surrounded by piles of Bibles and Lectionaries, quietly and without words, that Seth pulled Eirinn into their first kiss. It was dry, awkward, terrified Eirinn and was followed by an hour long embrace and a great deal of crying from Seth.

4

Eirinn eyes the road signs and map with suspicion, even though he plotted the course himself the night before. His directions to me are correct yet uncertain — he never changes his mind, but appears to be recalculating the path at every turn. Driving cross country chasing a stranger with his gay lover in the passenger seat is a new experience for me. He murmurs to himself as he looks over the map again and again. It is increasingly unsettling. It also stops me from continuing to ask questions.

I offer to navigate, and at the next rest stop, we switch seats. Eirinn welcomes the distraction and I easily call out directions, as there are few turns. The interview begins again, and has become a familiar rhythm for us after nearly a week on the road.

At the beginning of Seth's junior year, his teachers braced for the worst with his arrival. The mother who flew into class and stole away her kid, laughing in the teacher's face, was unsurprisingly the source of much gossip amongst the faculty, and every action of her child the source of much speculation, the fight especially so. When they heard of his mother's death they assumed he'd be a terror in class. They were surprised.

Seth never argued, or fought, or talked back. He did his homework, on time, and got good grades. When his new teachers conferred with his old ones, they were even more surprised — it seemed he was a better student since his mother's death. The teachers drew conclusions from their perspective.

Eirinn tells a different story.

"Junior year, Seth spent most of his energy trying never to speak to his father. He took on extracurriculars so he'd be home late, kept his grades up so there'd be no reason to yell, turned down going out so he wouldn't have to call his dad and ask permission."

"He told you this?"

"There was a crazy logic to it — he'd stay home on Saturdays, knowing his Dad would be there, because if he left he'd have to talk about where he was going. Even after all this, he still didn't come to my house."

"Was he angry at his father?"

Eirinn spits his response. "I don't psychoanalyze Seth. And that seems like a massive oversimplification, don't you think?"

This is the first Eirinn has spoken so openly or critically of Seth, or so defensively of his own actions. The tension in his voice is familiar; more than offending him, my question entirely missed the point.

He speaks faster, and pushes the pedal harder. I feel the acceleration in my gut, notice that we pass 80 on the speedometer, and debate whether to say anything, afraid I might break the spell and lose this rare open moment of unkind honesty.

"Did it work? How did his father react?"

"He seemed relieved. It was a two way street between them. Seth wanted to avoid speaking to him at nearly all costs, and Matthew seemed to be happy that Seth didn't need any help. I think when Katelyn died he was scared Seth would lose it. I certainly was. And I think he did, for a while. He was angry, a lot. He was violent a few times. But most of the time, it was like he wasn't even there. I started coming over without calling, because he wouldn't answer the phone. He wouldn't leave his room, and inside, he just sat. He would cry, he would sleep. For months after the funeral it didn't change."

Eirinn's frustration is visible. His eyes have widened and his grip tightened on the wheel. He sits forward in the seat, tense and scanning the horizon as quickly as he was scanning the map only an hour before.

"It was hard to watch."

His cellular phone vibrates — a missed call from his Dad comes through, as we pass a cell phone tower. He silences the phone. Eirinn pauses in pain, in nearly the strongest emotion I've seen him display the whole trip, and then makes the clear decision to tell me something he wasn't going to, another first.

"That's why I put him on antidepressants."

"You — you what?"

"I stole my dad's prescription pad and got Seth on antidepressants that summer. He was really bad, and I didn't know how to fix him. I was the only one he'd talk to and seeking help was absolutely out of the question — he wouldn't talk to his father about going out for dinner with friends, let alone seeing a psychiatrist. But I convinced him pills could help, and he listened."

"How long was he taking the pills?"

"He still is. Or was. I found a whole bottle that should have been used up at the house today. I think he's been off them for a while."

"Do you know what happens when you take those pills irregularly, or stop altogether?"

"I figured they just fade away."

I don't tell him what I know, that abruptly stopping antidepressants brings on a torrent of symptoms worse than the majority of the condition they were treating. My mother's dog tags suddenly weigh heavily on my neck, and I touch them through my shirt. I don't tell Eirinn what happened to my mother. My father would be disappointed. I don't know what my adviser would think.

"It was next to this."

Eirinn opens the glove compartment and pulls out a neon orange paper that's been crumpled into a ball. He unfolds it and reveals a cheaply made flyer, hand-drawn and then copied, advertising a group event. The date is weeks old, the group or event (the layout is unclear) is called "Following Shepard" and the only description given is "for gay men in need of direction, we are here."

"The address on it is our house."

I examine the flyer for meaning, but it escapes me. "What is it? What's Following Shepard?"

Eirinn's grip, already tight, shifts forward on the steering wheel. "I don't know. I don't remember anything happening on that date. I looked it up; it was a Wednesday, and I would have had class, but I don't remember seeing anyone unusual around the house then. More than Seth's friends who had started to hang out a lot, anyway."

Eirinn looks down at the speedometer and lets off the gas pedal suddenly. We slow down back to 65; he is quiet and I don't ask more questions. The spell is over.

5

On May 24, 1998, Matthew McCam moved to Italy to study theology and receive Holy Orders. He never completed his program, and in fact died 7 months later.

Matthew seems to be a man who was destined never to fulfill his destiny. As early as age 8, his parents remembered him showing a profound interest in faith. Thomas and Anna McCam have been gone for decades, but friends of the family still remember the story nearly word for word, of a young Matthew found with his father's rosary, praying on it in his room to be forgiven for stealing it in the first place.

Members of his childhood parish remember a dutiful altar server, carefully attentive to detail and once lovingly rebuked by the priest for trying to straighten the altar dressing in the middle of a sermon.

In high school, he officially declared his desire to be a priest on a form about his future plans. It appears as a side note on his permanent record. In his yearbook, there are few clubs, and even fewer inscriptions from friends.

The only stories anyone seems to tell of Matthew McCam before he turned 18 take place in the church, or holding one of its totems. His brothers declined comment.

Friends of Katelyn are mostly confused by the man — both by his presence and Katelyn's decision to marry him. They tell a story of a man who came to all the parties he knew Katelyn would attend, but never seemed to have a good time. The word dutiful pops up again, but among Katelyn's friends, it is no longer a compliment.

Matthew kept no journal of his life's events, or feelings about them. The paper trail of his life is mostly clerical — bills neatly organized in one drawer of a file cabinet, electronics manuals and warranty cards in another. His college diploma is framed, but in storage. Family photos show a man with a gentle smile, but he is in very few of them. In the attic are most of his possessions, by quantity and volume, boxed and roughly numbered, though the contents are in an order that is no longer possible to discern. Most were given away before the move to Rome, some were not.

There are 10 large boxes, too heavy to lift unaided, stuffed to the brim with books. Their weight, and the relative strength of the cardboard, implies that the books were brought up in small stacks and loaded into the boxes already in the attic. They are neatly stacked inside, packed like a 3 dimensional puzzle and wasting no space. None are rare, or priceless first printings, though several look old and well-worn.

At the top of box 5 is a copy of Matthew Lewis's The Monk, printed in 1952. Its spine is repaired with tape, now yellowed, and many pages are dog-eared — which makes it unique amongst Matthew's books. On the inside cover, there is an inscription: "Whatever you think about this book, you're wrong. Enjoy, K."

Page by page, warring treatises are squeezed tightly into the margins, illegible to anyone, save, I suspect, Matthew and Katelyn. The alternating handwriting and different writing utensils imply that the book was passed back and forth many times. Inside the back cover is a long list of dates in Matthew's script. They each match the writing utensil of a consecutive round of Matthew's counterpoints. The first one, January 7, 1969, is next to an inscription from Katelyn — "You're way too uptight." The dates continue, some days apart, some years, the last one dated March 17, 1996, is in Katelyn's handwriting. It predates her death by only a month, and fills the rest of the page with a note. "Please find somebody else to argue with, Matt."

A Paulist priest emerged late in my search for information about Matthew McCam. An old college friend, Father Park is surprisingly open. More than most of my interviewees, certainly more than anyone who can speak about Matthew McCam. There are permanent bags under his eyes. His hair is too gray, and his face is too wrinkled. He has endured tragedy, and it weighs on him.

"You know, I was at their wedding. I was one of the celebrants."

"One of? Who performed the ceremony?"

Park laughs, and it is surprising and powerful. "Well, Matthew was destined for the seminary — almost all of his friends were priests. So there were three of us on the altar. But there were also a dozen more in the pews."

He catches on to my surprise that Matthew had that many friends.

"Yes, Matthew was impressively introverted. But he had an amazing grasp of the study of faith. He was the guy everybody wanted to study with. In our small circle, he was popular. Outside of it, I don't think many people got to see what we did. Except Katelyn."

"How did they meet?"

"A debate. I don't remember who sponsored it. It was about the role of the church in modern society. Only as soon as Matthew and Katelyn began to talk they left everybody else behind. I'd never seen him so excited. I don't think he'd ever met anyone who could meet him toe to toe like that. She was always, always an amazing woman."

It is clear that Park suffered Katelyn's loss too.

"He changed. An introvert like Matthew, who'd always wanted to be a priest, had never sought out the attention of a woman. The landscape had changed and it did not take long for him to realize what that meant."

"And when she died?"

I don't intend to ask it then, but it's the question that's weighed heaviest — no one seems able to speak to what McCam was like after Katelyn's death.

"When he met her, a light turned on and opened up a new world for him to explore, and a life he never thought he would have. When she died, that light went out."

6

We pass a tower on our way toward Laramie and my cellular phone rings for the first time in our five days on the road. It's my adviser, and I debate heavily over whether to take the call. I e-mailed that I would be gone, chasing a story. In fact, I'd emailed all my professors at once and it suddenly occurs to me that they probably all called him. Answering this phone call suddenly seems a lot like visiting the principal's office.

Eirinn doesn't move his eyes from the map and the profile of his face is tense. The phone call is clearly making him nervous, but why or in what way is unclear.

Ultimately the decision is made for me — the signal fades after only a minute. My conscience gets to me at a gas stop 20 minutes later, however, and I stop at a pay phone. The shelf at the base of the phone is wooden and new, but still covered in scars. In the moments before I call him, the lattice of divots and scratches is intensely interesting.

"Will Orange."

"Hi. It's Mark."

"Hi Mark. Do you want to tell me what the hell you're doing out there?"

He's not yelling. In fact, I don't remember ever hearing him yell. His tone is the same jocular candor as always, and he's asking the same question as the time I took an extra hour taking campus pictures while looking for some candid shots.

"I'm chasing a story."

"About what?"

I've been gathering details, hours of conversation and notes from journals for nearly five days now. But something about talking to him forces me to summarize in a sentence.

"The freshman I mentioned, Seth McCam, disappeared about a week ago, and I'm with his best friend/boyfriend trying to chase him down."

"Where are you?"

"A gas station off Interstate 80, on our way into Laramie."

"You're in Wyoming? Mark, do you know what you're getting into?"

There is real surprise and concern in his voice, and it is unsettling. Both are rare, coming from him.

Dr. William Orange is an Associate Professor of Journalism at Johnstown University. He has three degrees in journalism, spent 9 years on active duty in the military and has lived 54 years. He has been married, raised two sons and lived in three countries, and still the most memorable moment of his life occurred at 23.

On assignment from his newspaper investigating police brutality, he went out in a patrol car with a pair of young cops. They chased down an armed murder suspect and he followed. When they cornered him, he opened fire — one officer shoved him out of the way, and took a bullet to the chest. The other was hit in the leg, but took the suspect down. William applied first aid, radioed for help and ultimately, saved the officer's life. When he went to the newspaper, his editor rejected the story saying he was too involved.

The next day, he enlisted in the army voluntarily and the story got him a spot in the press corps. It was 1968.

I don't know how to answer his question, so he continues to talk.

"Including you, Mark, there are at least 14 missing students right now, all of whom disappeared 7 days ago, around the same time as Seth McCam. Officially, nobody's noticed and the police won't get involved, because they're all supposed to be on a field trip to DC with the Straight Gay Alliance."

"Are they all playing hookie? An official group sponsored field trip would excuse them from classes."

"That's what the SGA adviser thought. But Mark, what do you know about Following Shepard?"

"Not much. Eirinn showed me this generic flyer he found. It seemed like they were some kind of gay exclusive support group, and they had met at his and Seth's house. He didn't seem to know about it."

"I've seen that flyer. I don't know what this group is, but I do know they've gone AWOL for a week and you're chasing them halfway across the country to Laramie, Wyoming."

"What's in —" I stop.

I remember the air in the newspaper office felt different on October 11, 1998. We were ashamed for feeling excited about our first national story to take the front page. We ran two pictures — a wire shot of the main vigil in Laramie, and one of our own on the quad. For the staff, it was emotionally rough, but I remember a quote from Edward Argent, one of the students at the vigil: "for us, it's more than sadness, it's terror. We live with the fear that asking the wrong person out will go past rejection into at best, disgust, and at worst, what happened to Matthew Shepard."

There's a gap between the glass and its metal framework. Outside the booth, Eirinn comes into focus through it, at that moment. His jacket is open and underneath is a suprisingly tight shirt — one he never intended to wear on this trip.

"Mark?"

"Yeah, I'm still here."

"What are you going to do?"

Journalists all have a moment in their careers when a story turns and they are faced with a decision. In covering the beat piece on city council meetings, you find out that a council member's brother is doing all the city's construction work. Do you investigate? The building next door is on fire. Do you grab pen and paper, or a bucket of water? For lucky journalists, that moment is early on, and they get to choose a new path if the news takes them places they don't want to go. When you discover, nearly a week into tracking him, that the man you're after is leading a dozen others to the site of somebody's murder and it makes you excited instead of terrified, you might not be a very good journalist, but your career path has already been decided.

"I'm going to Laramie."

"All right. Then there are three things you need to know."

"Number one: you're not invincible. What you are facing could be very real danger.

Number two: your responsibility is to the truth. Not the person in front of you."

He pauses a lot, so it's almost a full minute before I can tell he needs prompting.

"What's the third thing?"

"Oh. You're not excused from any of your classes. You should really get back soon."

7

Dillon and Meara Gallagher, who at the time had to pinch pennies to afford groceries, bought a solid oak dining room table and chair set in 1982 for $800, knowing they would not have a dining room to put it in until 10 years later. It has always been their prized possession.

Eirinn Gallagher was born in Ireland — but just barely. Dillon and Meara began making plans to emigrate from their home the moment they discovered Meara was pregnant. They both had lost family to guerilla fighting; the violence of The Troubles had been a constant reality of their adult lives. Growing up in Galway, the violence of the IRA and other groups never hit their home, but the ripple effects of the violence were inescapable throughout the Republic. When a child was to become a part of that reality as well, they knew Ireland could no longer be their home. Eirinn was born in Galway Regional Hospital. He was on a transatlantic flight less than a month later.

Eirinn grew up in a finished basement in the house of a cousin. It was one room, with curtains dividing the beds in the corner. Eirinn's bed was surrounded on two sides with a rolling curtain. The unfinished walls to the right and rear of the bed were cinder block, painted a cold, blue-white. The right wall has a small window that abuts the ceiling. It is such a small window at an odd angle that it only lets in sunlight a handful of days a year, for an hour at most. A few times, Eirinn tried to hang posters on the walls — but nothing ever stuck to the stone for very long.

The curtains separating the beds were on a rolling track — bought used from the hospital where Meara works, and installed by Dillon. They were movable, but Eirinn never rolled them back. Chains weighted the bottoms of the curtains and made them seem unnaturally stiff; even though there was never a breeze to move them.

They shared a kitchen and bathroom with the upstairs house, but rarely ate upstairs. For the Gallaghers, eating together is sacrosanct. For a family of three, Meara working all hours as a nurse, Dillon studying psychiatry and working part time, and Eirinn in varying hours of school and other projects, it wasn't always easy and dinner sometimes happened at odd hours. But with rare exception, the Gallaghers ate dinner together at their own table. It was cooked as often by Dillon as by Meara, with Eirinn stepping in to assist at an unusually early age.

To outsiders, the Gallagher family often appears cold. It takes time and a keen eye to see the affections of the Gallagher family. They hug infrequently. They are kind and express love, but it is quiet, and subtle. Issues in the family are discussed and debated; if they've ever had a shouting match, no one has ever seen it. But they are a family of occasion and gesture. Birthdays and holidays are celebrated with gifts that are surprisingly thoughtful. A gift from a Gallagher is never the most expensive one in the pile, but it is always the one most remembered by the recipient. And every year, Dillon and Meara agree that their gifts to each other should be replaced by a practical purchase for the family — yet no holiday goes by without presents exchanged between them.

In 1992, Dillon Gallagher opened his own psychiatry practice. Business went unusually well for a new practice. They moved into their own home a year later, in the summer between Eirinn's seventh and eighth grade.

It took all three of them to move the table, but Dillon would let no movers touch it. In the sunlight for the first time in 11 years, the table showed all its scratches, stains and dents, and there were many. Eirinn's usual place at the table was marked by an old water stain from when he was 8. He'd been grounded for three weeks for making it, but ever since, it had endeared him to that spot.

There was a deep, narrow gash in one corner that Dillon had made on Eirinn's fourth Christmas, carving a turkey with the family's first electric knife. There was a chip of wood missing from one of the ornate table legs from a misstep when Meara was carrying an old metal toolbox down the stairs. There was an 'E' carved on the bottom of one of the chair seats that Eirinn had made with his first pocket knife. He was never caught for that one.

Eirinn doesn't remember when his father taught him to ride a bike, or swim. He doesn't remember being taught to shave or tie a tie. But he does remember being taught to cook his own pizza dough, and he remembers the first three weeks in their new house, learning to refinish a table. They spent whole days together sanding it down, erasing the scars of its past.

It was the longest he had ever been alone in a room with his father. They didn't talk much, but it wasn't uncomfortable. Every once in a while, Eirinn would reload their drinks — he had a water, his father always a Diet Coke with three ice cubes. Dillon didn't ask for three, Eirinn just noticed that was what ran out at the speed his father drank them. Both father and son were a little surprised at the ease of their cooperation.

Eirinn was newly 13, and more and more of their relationship had become one big argument about nearly everything. It was natural, and Dillon knew it, but it was also unavoidable, and Dillon knew that too. But for the duration of those three weeks, they spent nearly every day in a room together only working.

Eirinn's reward came as a surprise, and immediately after. The entire family travelled to Ireland for a week, in what would become an annual tradition. In the Dublin airport, while his mother was in the restroom, Dillon shook his son's hand and said thanks for the hard work. When he pulled away, there were 500 Irish pounds in Eirinn's hand.

8

The population of Laramie sign is held up by wooden posts — I'm sure
it isn't the first such sign we've passed, but it's the first I've noticed. It's old
wood, cracked and weathered, but was rush treated with stain within the
last year. There are missed spots, and bad drip marks from a clearly rushed
job. Care was not taken in this work. Along the way, Eirinn has been
pointing these things out to me. Spotting quality wood care is like some
sort of superpower with him, and it appears to have rubbed off. At the
moment, his focus is pulled.

We have pulled off the road, just outside of Laramie. As we passed the sign,
Eirinn turned the atlas to the enlarged section of Laramie and was gravely
disappointed. Cheyenne and Casper take up most of the page — Laramie
is no more than a few roads in the corner. We have lost the trail. Eirinn still
scours the map, looking over the same dozen road lines as though this time
around they will hold some new secret.

We drive into town, and Eirinn's tension continues to rise. He is craned
forward looking for a gas station, a book store, something that will have a
map of Laramie. The tiny racks in each location hold nothing — and when
he asks the clerks, they chuckle at the idea of needing a map for their town,
and ask him where he needs to go. Eirinn's noncommittal noises get quieter
in each store, as the conversation plays on repeat.

On March 29, 1999 at 11:30 a.m., I was alone on duty; I picked up the phone in the office of The Light, our student newspaper. Eirinn was on the other end. The phone conversation was short, he asked me to come to an off-campus coffeehouse for a story. I met him a half-hour later, when my shift was up.

The coffeehouse was full of students deep in books and couples deep in each other's eyes; Eirinn was not hard to pick out. He wore a button down shirt and khakis, and a pea coat hung on his chair. The clothes themselves didn't set him apart, but their coordination and the pressed shirt lied about the condition he was in. The coffee, in a small cup held tight in his hands, was already cold. It was clear from the cup in front of him that he hadn't moved since our phone call.

He was still, staring somewhere beyond the window. I had to sit down at the table to draw his attention.

"Mark?" he asked.

"Yeah."

"You'll probably want to get some coffee before we, um, before we start."

"I don't drink coffee."

He looked down into his drink and chuckled.

"You're missing out."

I set my tape recorder on the table.

"Is this okay? I'm terrible at taking notes without it."

He nodded. The tape started with a click. He looked up at me. He didn't ask me to travel with him for another twenty minutes, but it was in the moment his eyes looked into mine that I said yes. I didn't need to know the question. There was so much need, so much hope pouring out of them. I was on the receiving end of a prayer.

_____

Those same eyes look up at me now.

"He's gone to the fence, I'm sure of it. I just — I don't know where it is. And I don't know how to find it."

Journalism ethics are complicated. There are a few obvious rules: don't lie, always fact check, and don't interfere with the story. But there's a reason the subject takes up an entire class, that I hadn't taken at the time, in serious journalism programs. The right paths to take, as a journalist or human being, often lead off in opposite directions, and are hard to decipher in the first place. In March 1993, a photojournalist named Kevin Carter working in Sudan photographed a starving toddler trying to reach a feeding center. He did not aid the girl because he was told touch could transmit disease. The photo appeared in the New York Times and hundreds of other papers, spreading awareness on a global scale. That August, the US added Sudan to the list of state sponsors of terrorism. He won the Pulitzer prize in April 1994, and committed suicide three months after that. Carter never learned what happened to the girl in the photograph. It is hard, on the ground, to know what to do. You have a moment to decide and the consequences can change your life. Depending on your circulation, It can also change a thousand others.

We are standing in a gas station parking lot, and the pavement is coarse and irregular. Bits of the asphalt have broken into gravel, scattered by our drive here, but the pattern of tiny stones and black tar remains unchanged. Through the window of the station, the attendant goes back and forth, watching us or the TV in the corner. There's nothing else for him to do in there.

I've come at this a hundred different ways, and there are at least as many rationales to justify my decision to help him, but I'd be lying if I claimed a single one of them flitted through my head as I told him to head to the library. I only looked into his eyes.

At the coffeehouse, when I agreed to travel with Eirinn, a moment of what I thought was relief had passed over his face before his mind immediately filled up with minute details. He wouldn't ask those questions for a couple hours; he didn't know me well enough yet, but they were speeding through his mind.

Seeing that same change play across his face again I can place the expression; one of both relief and dread. We are once again barreling forward toward answers. But Eirinn is more keenly aware than anyone that they are answers he may not want to find.

9

The library was a bust. I'd been searching for copies of the Laramie Boomerang or the Branding Iron (University of Wyoming student paper), but the paper copies had been thrown out and the microfilm wouldn't be available for another 5 years. The only answer we got out of people, as though it were scripted, was that the fence where Matthew Shepard was murdered was "on private property."

I got the impression most of them had been asked before.

We've been in the police station for half an hour. I gave Seth's name, over Eirinn's objection, and mentioned we were looking for a group at the fencepost. The chairs are uncomfortable, the officer at reception wary of our questions, the whole room is badly in need of a paint job — these are all things I expected. The coffee, the smile of the other officer who brought it, and the lounge he takes us to are surprises. I refuse my cup. He offers to return with tea, and I thank him. Alone in the lounge, Eirinn notices a lingering, questioning look from me to the door.

"He's family."

It takes me a minute to understand. Once I do, I can't help but be distracted by it.

"How do you know?"

Eirinn stares into his coffee in a familiar way.

"A few things. His face. His smile. His pants."

"But they're uniform pants."

"They've been taken in a size in a few places."

He doesn't look up from his coffee.

"I just notice these things."

I'm defensive at the condescension in his voice. "I've heard of gaydar, Eirinn. Is yours any good?"

"Yes."

His coffee is far too hot to drink, but he clasps the styrofoam with both hands and breathes the drink in, his eyes closed and head bowed. He breathes slow and deep; the rhythm of his breath visible in the steam. He is quiet.

The officer returns quickly with a cup of hot water and an old Lipton tea bag. He must be 35, and I consider what that means for a gay man who's grown up to be a police officer in Laramie Wyoming. I can't imagine choosing that life. But he shares another kind smile and looks me in the eye.

"We didn't have a lot of selection."

"Thanks."

His eyes turn to Eirinn as he sits down across from him. I still don't see it; he looks straight to me. But somehow I pick up that I, in turn, look straight to him. So much of the conversation that follows I don't grasp. From the cop's expression, I doubt I'm meant to.

"Tell me about Seth."

On what might have been the most important night of his life, Seth McCam fell asleep in the Cathedral of the Holy Father. It may have been that he was attending a midnight mass on Christmas eve, it may have been the nearly unbearable headache he was suffering from. It may have been the fact that he was exhausted from an irreconcilable fight he had just had with his father. No one is sure.

In fact, no one is quite sure whether he fell asleep, passed out or fainted. But as the incense passed by him in the processional, Eirinn Gallagher saw him lose consciousness. Eirinn's best church-quiet efforts could not rouse Seth, and he was not about to risk garnering the attention of the now-packed cathedral. Instead he sat and focused on the deacon leading the processional.

Eirinn was bored out of his mind. He felt underdressed in his polo shirt and black pants. He felt out of place between the vaulted arches. He didn't go to church. His family was at home in bed, where he had left them after dinner. They didn't go to church. His family hadn't gone together for at least a year. The only reason he was here was now dripping on the stone floor.

Eirinn looked closer. It wasn't drool. A steady stream of tears had carved an odd pattern down to his chin. His nose, meanwhile, was draining into his mouth. Eirinn took advantage of the parishioners standing to begin the service and shook Seth, who groaned. He sat up.

Seth was pallid. He clung to Eirinn as he was led down the central aisle to the back of the church and out. Seth made it three steps out the door before vomiting on the cathedral steps. His head and gullet a little clearer, Seth walked to the car leaning on Eirinn.

Seth would not say much, but he refused the hospital. He clutched his head in the car. Eirinn gave him Aspirin for the pain and peppermint for the nausea. He didn't know if it would help, but he had to do something.

They made it home without further incident. Inside, Eirinn took care of everything. He lay Seth down in bed and lay a warm washcloth on his forehead, massaging him gently until the redhead fell asleep. Then he went downstairs and cleared the evening's dishes, sweeping away the shards of a broken tumbler and the dirt tracked in through the kitchen back door. Eirinn turned out the lights, returned Seth's washcloth to the bathroom, kissed him on the forehead, and joined him in bed.

The body of Matthew McCam was buried 20 feet away, in the back yard.

37

In response to the officer's request, Eirinn says nothing. The officer doesn't look at me, only stares at the top of Eirinn's bowed head for a long moment.

"Come on. I'll take you to the fence."

After five days of traveling, the last leg of our journey following Seth McCam takes 12 minutes in the back of a cop car. Eirinn says nothing. The officer says nothing. I am watching them both, and the road, and trying to ignore my racing heartbeat.

When we arrive at the scene, I am frozen. Other things happen, but the only thing I will remember from our arrival is thinking I've never seen that much blood before.

10

The following article ran in The Light on April 7, 1999.

Dateline, Laramie, Wyoming April 4 — 11 JU students were found dead, and one critically injured, now in a coma, on a ranch at the same fence where University of Wyoming Student Matthew Shepard was found only six months earlier. Each of the deceased students had identical wounds: shallow cuts on the palms of their hands, apparently self-inflicted.

Marijuana, Phencyclidine (PCP) and cyanide were present at the scene. The full coroner's report has not yet been released to the public, but representatives of the Laramie police department have assured that "the cause of death has been ascertained, and the investigation is ongoing."

The police statement went on to confirm that drugs were involved in the deaths, but did not release any details in regards to their usage or which students may have been intoxicated.

The comatose student, Seth McCam, was severely beaten. According to Mark Tabari, a JU student present at the initial discovery, he was found, arms and body tied to the post, with bruises scattered over his body. In addition to the same cuts as the deceased students, he was cut across the forehead and wrists.

Matthew McCam, Seth's father, has been missing for nearly four months, a fact only discovered after recent attempts to contact him about his son's condition. Police officials in Rome, where Matthew had been studying for priesthood, report that he left to spend Christmas with his son in America, and never returned, instead writing a letter resigning his position in the school.

The deceased students have been identified as Arthur Pascal, Jamie Boanerges, Andi Patras, Flip Bolani, Nathan Tanner, Sean Davidson, Castor Patel, Jamie Miner, Barney Joseph, Sawyer Kana and Edward Argent. As of press time, all of their families had been contacted by both a representative of the Laramie police department and JU President Dr. Toby Butcher.

Butcher made a statement to the press Monday, saying "The JU community is shocked and saddened by the events of Sunday, April 4. Our hearts and my prayers are with the families and loved ones of those we have lost."

The statement also said that a task force would be formed to investigate the possibility that Johnstown resources were used in the process. All 12 of the deceased students found were members of the Straight Gay Alliance (SGA), an official student group organized to "educate the JU community on GLBTQIQSS issues," according to their charter.

The 12 students found in Laramie were scheduled to be on a field trip to Washington, DC, along with several other students whose names are not being released. The purpose of the field trip was to attend a protest in support of hate crimes legislation. According to SGA Adviser Barb Kerzenmacher, the students disappeared after the first day of the trip. "We handed out the per diem cash at the first rest stop, and the cars carrying those students turned around and drove the other way. We reported the theft to the University immediately."

The 12 students also attended meetings of an unofficial group called Following Shepard. Meetings of Following Shepard began at least two months ago, taking place at Seth McCam's house.

On Thursday, the Campus Christian Fellowship (CCF) plans to hold a candlelight vigil for the deceased students and Seth McCam. "We are still learning what happened in Laramie, Wyoming," said CCF president Frank Baker, "but we know for certain those students are in need of our prayers now." The vigil will take place on the quad at 8 p.m.

41

Eirinn and I had a five day journey chasing Seth and the members of Following Shepard across the country. I have reported that story from my own firsthand experiences, and the past events were recreated from interviews and verified whenever possible.

The rest of the story is recreated entirely by interview and research. In some cases, events are recreated from the testimony of only one or two sources, the only surviving witnesses to the events. Whenever possible, testimony was checked against documentation and factual research.

11

Seth empties the chips into a bowl and toys nervously with the empty bag. He is accustomed to parties but not to hosting them in his home — it's not something his family ever did. Childhood birthdays were spent at Chuck E. Cheese, or private rooms in restaurants when he got older. The house is certainly equipped for sizeable parties — Eirinn believes it was at the insistence of Seth's grandparents, since Katelyn always booked venues for her gatherings, and Matthew never seemed to bring anyone home. Up until Matthew moved out, the expansive living room furniture seemed to exist only for the maid to clean once a month.

Eirinn is at an evening class and halfway across campus. Seth hasn't told him about Following Shepard; he isn't really sure why. It weighs on his mind as he rearranges the bowls for the third time. The timing of tonight weighs on his mind too: outside it is already dark, and extremely cold. He considers that attendance tonight might be a lot to ask. Then suddenly, Seth wonders if he has enough food.

Eirinn is nearly the only friend of Seth's who has ever seen his house. For a lot of people, college is the first time to have likeminded people over to discuss shared interests. For Seth, it was also the first time he'd had friends over, in plural. Andi Patras and Arthur Pascal are the first to arrive and begin the first meeting of Following Shepard.

The JU Straight Gay Alliance was first recognized by the student senate as an official organization on October 21, 1996. The vote was 22-17 in favor, with 6 senators absent and 2 abstaining. Barb Kerzenmacher said she considers the day to be a "big win for LGBT students of JU." Though she was not allowed by rules of order to speak before the Senate, she faculty sponsored the organization's petition for membership and was "proud of her part in the creation of the group." The quote is from a speech she gave at a celebration event afterwards, which she organized. She recited the speech to me during our interview.

The SGA remains the only official group catering to gay students in JU history. Kerzenmacher had been pushing for its creation since her first day as a faculty member in 1992, but received a dramatic increase in support when a Spring 1995 survey of graduating Seniors, the first to ever ask about student sexual orientation (on Kerzenmacher's insistence), found that less than 10% of students identifying as gay said they "enjoyed their time at JU." They also were 4 times more likely than the student body to say that JU did not "accomodate their needs as a student" or "foster a safe and open learning environment." The latter two items troubled many faculty members; the former is the most likely indicator of whether students will donate to the school as alumni.

Barb Kerzenmacher is a woman who always seems to be smiling, except when she is not. At our first meeting, she wore a great deal of denim — light blue, high waisted jeans with large pockets, and a matching vest with embroidered characters sewn in the front. Her hair is very short, brown and beginning to grey, and kept in meticulous order without the assistance of gel or hair spray. Small talk and short order conversation are easy with her: she can hold a conversation about nothing at all for a very long time and with remarkable ease. Disagree with her, and a different woman emerges.

I asked, in our second and final meeting, why she thought the students of Following Shepard left. Nearly everyone I asked answered "I don't know." Students I asked have all responded with confusion, and faculty with sadness. Kerzenmacher seemed only to respond with anger. To her, my question was an accusation, and clearly not a new one. She straightened her posture, her smile soured, and I am still fairly certain I saw her hair stand up straighter. After this change, the conversation is over. This, I suspect, is

45

the woman who permanently ejected three students from her trigonometry class for using the word faggot, at no one in particular.

Kerzenmacher is a JU alumna from the class of 1988, and says that JU during her time as a student was "a different place. We used to organize 'blue jeans days,'" she said, "where students would be encouraged to wear jeans to identify as a supporter of gay or lesbian rights." She says she remembers personally seeing at least three people run back to their rooms to change out of jeans after being told what was going on. She says it without a smile.

On May 13, 1998, Joann Bianchi, a straight Junior Early Childhood Education major, defeated Andi Patras in an election for president of the SGA for the 1998-1999 school year. The vote count is known only to Kerzenmacher, who counted them, but nearly all the members of the Straight Gay Alliance seem to think it was a landslide. On September 14, the third president of the SGA was late to the group's first meeting of the year. Andi was not.

Jamie Boanerges and Aras Fisher arrive at the McCam house only moments after Andi and Peter, yet when Seth opens the door, they are greeted with a charming smile. The five are immediately, naturally and completely at ease with each other. Seth's living room could seat 12, comfortably in chairs and couches around the room. Yet the five are huddled closely together, Andi the only one on an easy chair with Arthur in front of him, leaning back against his legs. Jamie, Aras and Seth form the rest of a tight circle, seated on the floor and close enough that everyone is overlapping. They're having such a good time, nobody even brings up the failings of the SGA for half an hour. Once on the subject, however, they don't leave it until three hours later.

12

It is January 18, 1999 at 6:45 p.m. the Straight Gay Alliance is about to have its first meeting of the quarter, and Joann Bianchi is early, for only the third time in her tenure as president. She puts on her glasses and reviews the agenda — she has a lot to talk about.

It's because she's wearing them that she notices a group of her male members whispering outside — in their black coats, they look like a cluster of floating heads. One of them, it looks like Sean Davidson, makes brief eye contact then looks away. The door is unlocked, so she's uncertain why they don't just come inside. At least, until she sees Arthur Pascal.

Ever since he lost the election, Andi Patras has been quiet at meetings and civil to Joann. Both are unprecedented. She'd be able to think he's over it, except Arthur, whom she never sees without him, can't seem to stop hating everything she does. She goes to the door and beckons everyone in from the cold. Somebody murmurs "we thought it was locked," and she brushes it off. When the group of four sit in the farthest corner from her and continue a pointedly private conversation, she brushes it off too.

Over the next ten minutes, about 15 more people filter in to the Multicultural House. There's no confirmed record. At every meeting, it is reaffirmed that signing in is totally optional, and that being on the e-mail list is totally anonymous, even to other members. At this meeting, Joann tops a sign-in list of 6 people, including Andi Patras, Arthur Pascal, Barb

Kerzenmacher and Frederick Hahn. Hahn is a small, effeminate man, the other faculty adviser of the SGA.

Joann welcomes everyone to the meeting and quickly dispenses with old business. She reiterates, before Jamie Miner can bring it up again, that the group will not make a field trip to a gay club or gay bar — even if they let in people under 21. Students may undertake that on their own.

New business at this meeting is what she's most excited about, but it's also where things always go off the rails. The AIDS charity drive discussion goes smoothly, at least — the theatre department is putting on a production and the SGA is co-sponsoring (not to mention makes up half the cast) and nobody objects.

It's the Valentine's day plans where things fall apart, and it surprises her. Joann, knowing that most of her members had been disenfranchised by or even thrown out of their high school proms, had decided to put together a Valentine's day dance. When she brings up the idea, even Andi seems on board — but he and the members hanging outside before the meeting object to every detail.

The location of the multicultural house — too small and not enough room to dance, even though they've never filled it for a meeting or event. The date, February 18, set to avoid a series of sorority balls, in which she and a few other members are involved — they accuse her of not putting the SGA first. But the advertisement method: e-mails only to the SGA e-mail list are what cause the loudest objectors to be silent, even though she knows they have the biggest objection. They've covered this issue before.

On May 5, 1998, the SGA sponsored a showing of Out of the Past, a documentary about forming a Gay-Straight Alliance at a Salt Lake City high school. It was shown in one of the large ballrooms in the student center, with over 150 chairs set up. Three people attended.

On April 16, 1998, a special meeting was held to determine the advertisement of the film showing. Caleb Felton, the president at the time had decided not to allow the film to be advertised with flyers around the student center, as was customary. In an e-mail to the group about the event, he said that, in order to ensure there were no "negative, inappropriate comments" during or after the movie, that the film would only be advertised via the SGA e-mail list. Patras and two other students strongly objected over e-mail, and Felton asked the advisers to help saying he was "in over his head." Kerzenmacher e-mailed Patras and the members who had objected inviting them to a meeting.

Andi Patras, arriving at the meeting, found himself surrounded by 8 faculty members, the Director of Residence Life and 3 group members including Bianchi and Felton, all in support of not using flyers. Only Patras, Edward Argent, and Miranda Flores, the three students who had e-mailed complaints, were in support of using flyers.

Flores, an SGA member of the class of 1998, described it a year later, and was not calm about it. "It was an ambush, plain and simple. We came in expecting a discussion, wanting to talk about it and willing to compromise. They only wanted to show us why they were right and if we didn't agree, that there was nothing we could do about it."

"Caleb Felton started by introducing the issue, but after that it was pretty much just a back and forth between whatever adviser was standing up to throw the punch at Andi and me, though Ms. Kerzenmacher definitely took the lead. We tried to tell them — to get them to understand, that what we were asking for was no more than any other group. That the whole reason to show a documentary was to get people talking, and they only wanted to invite the choir to preach to. They switched arguments a lot — sometimes that we didn't understand the harshness of the JU environment, how it used to be and how far we've come. Almost all of them made the 'don't think I'm prejudiced, I have gay friends' argument. And I think it was because we were getting increasingly angry."

Felton and Flores both recall that the breaking point was one faculty member saying that "they need to protect and create a safe space for people who are afraid to stand up and be counted, as you are."

Patras began to shout in response. "Fuck them! They're holding up the cause. I'm sick of neutering this group, watching everything we do, dilluting myself and my identity, just to create a safe space for anonymous cowards who never show up."

49

Both Felton and Flores recall the monologue word for word. They also agree it lost Andi the election.

Bianchi was the next person to speak in the meeting, by calling it to a close and thanking everyone for coming. She was calm and graceful. Flores says that "Andi always thought it was rehearsed."

When Joann mentions the advertisement methods of the Valentine's dance, there's a tension the freshmen don't understand. Kerzenmacher stands before she addresses everyone.

"Joann and I have discussed it, and we feel that advertising only to our members is the best way to make sure the event only attracts people who will enjoy themselves."

Less than a half hour passes before the living room in Seth's house is alive with the excited chatter of nine gay men. They belong, all of them; each of them. There is an instant understanding that most of them, the freshman especially, have never felt. For every boy in this room, high school conflated self-discovery with isolation. Each new trait, each new feeling that emerged only served to widen the gulf to their peers, until this room. Here anger does not need explanation. Here experiences are already shared. In this room, everyone is on a first name basis with Ellen. In this room, everyone is already tired of Will & Grace's cliches — but still never misses an episode. What is obscure, forced and misunderstood in the rest of their lives is the native language of each person they talk to here.

It's been five days since Following Shepard's first meeting of four. In two days, they'll begin meeting almost daily, in some form or another. The belonging is intoxicating, and innocent enough, at first.

13

Amongst the three of them on the video, there is no doubt who is in control. To an outsider, it is much less obvious. Physically, Sawyer seems the most intimidating. He's 6'4" and 200 lbs with a body carved from strenuous exercise and careful diet. The tallest of the three, if this were a wrestling match (which it often resembles) he would be the easy winner. Yet he always willingly submits to uncomfortable, even painful looking positions. Edward on the other hand, the shortest and smallest, always seems to wind up on top.

The Lima, OH gay bar is an unobtrusive building, almost hidden to the passive observer. From the outside it almost looks like an odd shaped house — it even has the slatted aluminum siding typical of the area. The sign out front, "Somewhere in Time", is all black-and-white, and a city silhouette — I'm told it's a hint, as are the blacked out windows. Inside is what I would call a unique decor. Edward Argent would disagree, as he recounted in his journal.

> "No two small town gay bars are, strictly speaking, the same, but they all have a great deal in common. They all have a theme which was abandoned at one point or another — the higher the lesbian population, the sooner. In fact, the more lesbians that go to the bar, the more it feels like a communal pub. I haven't done the math, but

my guess is you could gauge the size of the lesbian v. gay patronage by the respective square footages of the booths and the dance floor — essentially every small town gay bar has both."

Somewhere in Time, the full name of which is "Somewhere in Time When Even The Moon is Not Enuff," has two seperate and distinct sections — a long bar with tables and booths, and a dance floor in the next room. Argent's statements seem accurate as far as Somewhere is concerned — at one point old movies seem to have been a theme, but there are news articles scattered on the walls amongst the old movie posters. Occasionally two adjoining walls are painted the same color, but there is no cohesive color scheme to the place. The dance floor, and adjoining stage, has a cage on it. There is a jukebox shoved to the side on the bar side, a dart board squeezed in near the entrance and a pool table in an odd-shaped area in back.

At one point, it's just Sawyer and Nathan. Their heights are not so different — Nathan is only a few inches shorter, but the contrast is still stark. Nathan is skin and bones. There is a faint outline of muscle across his frame, but they are only apparent because there is barely an ounce of fat anywhere on his body. His ribcage is more visible than his abs. Yet again, Sawyer is pushed into ever more awkward positions as Edward steps off camera, though it's not clear who all knows that it's there. They're in Edward's bedroom, but he is very drunk and neither Nathan nor Sawyer appear to be. It seems unlikely, however, they could be unaware of the camera.

"It's not suprising this happens to small town gay bars. Each one has to be a pub to meet and talk with old friends, a dance club, a drag stage, and a full bar. In small towns, there's only one — in truly small towns, you have to drive to the one an hour away. It has to tailor to young twinks, old lesbians, middle-aged bears and everything in-between."

Argent describes these places dispassionately, though he apparently spent a great deal of time in them. Members of the SGA, in varying numbers and composition, visited Somewhere at least once a week, with only occasional breaks when a dance club in Kenton had a gay night. Argent usually supplied transportation, with the deal that someone else was designated driver on the return trip. In his journal, Argent makes mention of these trips as though they are his service to the community, offering transportation to "the only place within 100 miles where it is safe to be gay." But most accounts say it is simply Argent finding a way to establish a permanent designated driver arrangement. Whichever is the case, Argent is barely exaggerating. After Somewhere, the next nearest gay bar to JU is 90 minutes away.

The only other option, the dance club in Kenton, has a gay-themed night once a month. JU is located in a small town — a village, technically. But comparatively, there are 6 straight bars within its limits, 5 restaurants, not including the 7 pizza places. And on any given weekend, at least 4 different fraternities are hosting open parties that don't even require a fake ID. All are within walking distance of the JU dormitories. And every gay student I interview has stories showing that these are not safe spaces to show affection.

One pair of boys held hands at a restaurant and was asked to leave. One pair of girls kissed at a pizza place and left after frat boy hooting did not cease for 3 minutes. When he wore drag to one of the bars, one boy was harassed by other patrons — and then thrown out by the owner.

 Edward finishes first and seems quickly disinterested in everything else. Within a minute he is asleep. Nathan and Sawyer take care of each other quickly and lay down to sleep on either side of Edward. The video stops shortly after, though nobody appears to shut it off. It may be because a new recording was made over it. Immediately after the conclusion, another scene begins — there are 5 on the tape in total. Nathan appears in four of them, Sawyer in 3. The videos are shot in several different locations over the course of several months, and it is never clear who is filming them — but the video camera belongs to Barney Joseph.

14

Seth is standing in the McCam living room, the 10 current members of Following Shepard sitting in front of him, their eyes hungry. Jamie Boanerges is sitting closest, but it hardly matters. They're all close together on the floor, practically intertwined, except for Andi and Edward, on easy chairs behind. The seating arrangements are a pattern, or part of one. They hang on Seth's words, and in an hour even Edward will be able to repeat them with remarkable consistency.

> "They want our love. They want to steal it, shape it and not return it until it's deformed beyond recognition. Our fathers deny us their love. Our mothers fear our love for each other. And they believe they can strip from us the love of God.
> Men of the inconstant cloth chip away at our love. They stab, strike and banish it, and of their words a fire is born among the flock. They have put us to that fire for millennia and would again, but for all their efforts we are fire-hardened. We are now immune. Their fences will not hold us, their fire will not burn us, their weapons break against our skin. We are stone. We are carved in the image of God by the torments of His devils.
> Our inquisitors are not so tempered. When we strike back with their own fire, they will burn to ashes."

Jamie Boanerges was given a gift for his baptism at 14: a white, leather-bound blank book with silver leaf lettering: My Journey with Jesus in the center, James Boanerges at the bottom right. The inside cover records the baptism: Holy Fire Church, August 12, in the year of our Lord 1995. The entries are undated, florid and plentiful.

In the nearly five years of the journal, Jamie's faith took his thoughts to many places. He sought refuge in other virtues, in constant prayer, in a void of all temptation. If his journal is to be believed, Jamie never even masturbated until college. Across these patterns, it's still clear that Jamie knew what he was; he comes back to the same point again and again.

Sometimes it is his only true sin, sometimes his original sin. In the journal, his desire for men goes by many names, but it is always at the center of his struggle. At times, he seems to believe he will beat it — reach a point where it will permanently no longer trouble him. But these feelings disappear in the last 6 months of entries. In the last month, the entries stop referring to his sex as sin at all.

Jamie's journal mentions that Andi Patras introduced him to both Aras and Seth. It gives the actions one sentence a piece, and two pages to the meeting of each. Jamie's entries have been sexual before, but in prior entries, the desire always subdued to his shame.

Jamie is intoxicated by Aras. The entry made after their first meeting, which included sex, is a moment by moment description of the experience. Shame came and went and came again later, but the night of their first meeting is conspicuously free of it.

Jamie met Seth, in the second meeting of Following Shepard, three days later. From the moment they met, Jamie idolized him. To Jamie, Seth was someone who had done the impossible in reconciling his faith with his sexuality. In the description of their first meeting, Seth is described as a teacher. Within a week, he is upgraded to prophet.

"They fear the truth that I know. That you must know. That our love is greater than theirs. Each of them come from different worlds, they inhabit different bodies. They were born apart and spend a life trying to be together. They can never join as we do. We were born of one body. When many of us join, we are still one body."

"In whatever order we choose, whatever manner we decide, we may join in the same body. Our love is greater than theirs. They can exile us from our homes, burn us at the stake, and bury our secrets in the ground, but they can never touch our heart. For millenia we have found each other, in every nation. They have fought, for two thousand years, in the falsehood of His name, to exterminate us, but we have only ever grown back stronger and better. We are proof of the true nature of the world."

The true religious convictions of the rest of Following Shepard will never be known for certain. Edward Argent recorded several of the speeches in his own journal. He calls them sermons, but may have been sarcastic. Aras Fisher did not himself believe, but was convinced that everyone else did. Castor Patel describes the events as religious experiences, but his journal never conveys religious authority onto Seth.

There is precise record of the words Seth spoke. But what meaning they had for the members of his audience was lost with their deaths. They were kept at rapt attention; they were comforted, excited and driven to action by the speeches. But Jamie Fisher is the only one we know took them to be the Word of God.

Seth finishes speaking and sets down his leather-bound journal. Inside is a complete transcription of his words, written in pencil free from eraser marks. The outline of his thumb remains pressed into the book's cover, where he held it closed the entire time. The groove is deep, and now dark and ringed with the same fresh sweat that glistens on Seth's face. His face is flushed and his smile persistent.

When Andi slinks to the front of the room and brushes his hand, Seth follows him and Arthur up to the master bedroom, nearly panting. Nathan and Flip adjourn to Seth's old bedroom. Sex fills the McCam house. There's a couple in nearly every room, feeding off each others' noise. In the basement, Aras has Jamie pinned against the concrete wall. It scratches him and no matter how long his body is against it, the stone is a freezing cold that bites at his skin.

Jamie seems driven by the noise from upstairs. He is possessive and commands with his hands and eyes. Words don't pass his lips; they aren't needed. Others in the house are screaming, and something breaks upstairs, but Aras loses track of the world as Jamie opens his pants.

Eirinn is across campus in an extended physics lab. He won't be home for two more hours, and the messes will be cleaned up by then, at least in the master bedroom.

The sex isn't new, neither is the presence of so many members of Following Shepard. For Eirinn, their presence is neither particularly welcome nor suspicious. The sex, however, would be news to him. He has never been informed, or invited. Though their presence is annoying, it seems perfectly natural that so many students would escape the strict rules and cramped rooms of the dormitory for the house of a friend.

15

A good samaritan attempts to wake Castor before the end of class. Two taps and a light shove turn out to be the limit of his charity, but it is enough to remind Castor to pack up and be ready to leave by the lecture's end.

Castor walks slowly and stumbles twice on his way to the McCam house. Nathan Tanner lets him in, but the house is otherwise deserted. Nathan helps him up the stairs to the spare bedroom.

Gravity pulls Castor's pants to the floor once Nathan removes his belt. He isn't slow, or gentle, but Castor doesn't stop him as his hands are bound with the belt.

In his own words, nine months before his death, Castor Patel believed all he really needed was "the kiss of true love, or at least somebody hot."

Castor kept a LiveJournal, with the username doubtingthomas, which he entered in 4-5 times a week. The entries vary in length, but not in content. They're a repository for his loneliness and isolation — more emotion than a log of his life. There are few comments on each entry — he doesn't seem to have much readership. Yet they all close with the provocative "flames keep my feet warm at night."

The LiveJournal is the only substantial record of his character still standing. Castor was an only child, and after his death his parents left the country.

No friends stepped forward from high school, and all the ones from college were at the fence in Laramie. Even the survivors of that road trip are only able to describe him with broad strokes and physical details. They know for certain that he clung to Edward Argent.

Castor's first kiss and first sexual encounter happened within about 15 minutes of each other, and both were with Edward Argent. Castor didn't tell Edward he was a virgin, but his inexperience must have been obvious to Edward, four years his senior. Argent must have known the event meant more to Castor than it did to him. The story of the event is the longest entry on Castor's livejournal account — Argent's journal makes no mention of it.

When Edward arrives at the McCam house, Castor is asleep again. Nathan is prone on the couch, his head in Flip's lap. He's smiling as Flip strokes his hair. At Edward's appearance, the smile shifts into a smirk. At Nathan's smirk, Edward knows to head upstairs.

He finds Castor, still bound to the bed, still clothed from the waist up, now asleep, impressive given his uncomfortable position. Edward is gentle removing the belt, but it still wakes the supine figure. His lips tighten at the state of Castor's wrists. They've been bound before. There are marks and rug burns, none too old, but not all young. Castor tries not to retract when Edward touches them gingerly.

No words are exchanged, no sounds but regular breathing nearly covered by the shifting sheets are heard in the room as Edward lays down behind Castor. He spoons the shorter boy and strokes his hair.

Edward was a Junior at JU when Castor came to school. About him, people say a lot more. "He always needed to be the smartest person in the room. Sometimes he did it by sitting in a corner, looking superior. But if you ever wanted him to talk, you only had to lightly challenge his superiority. Cite a fact he knew was wrong and he'd leap to correct you. Claim you were an expert in anything he wasn't and he'd strive to discredit the whole field. Speak on a topic he knew nothing about and he'd change the subject."

His TAs were not his biggest fans.

Edward kept a journal himself, bound of cold-pressed paper in obvious signatures, with glass panels at the front and back. The book is less than a quarter full, the entries are not dated and they are rarely biographical. Each page reads more like an opinion column or rant. Edward had a lot of ideas about the future of gay people and society, and more than the occasional pun.

Before most people you ask tell you that Edward was short, or his hair and eyes were brown, they'll tell you he was an old man before his time. College life at JU had no shortage of immaturities to scoff at, but Edward seemed to go out of his way to find them in order to turn up his nose. At parties occupied exclusively by the t-shirt and flannel clad, he was the one exception in an Oxford button-down.

Castor's journal is nearly the only account of Edward's kindness, and by all appearances, the only person he was ever so kind to — even his own journal makes no mention of his caring for the younger boy, save a few references to a 'fatter boy, a marked recipient of the internalized cruelty of the gay community.'

While his own kindness toward Castor was undocumented, the boy's journey was spelled out in more detail. Edward suspected he wasn't eating. Castor and Aras were the only two overweight members of Following Shepard. Of the two, Castor was skinnier, but more sensitive as well. Edward estimates Castor lost 20 lbs over the months of Following Shepard.

> "He knows he isn't the way gays are supposed to look. I doubt straight men train their eyes to the mirror so harshly. In a fraternity, the boy would be in the middle of weight classes. But in a house of manicured fit men, he is ugly and fat."

It's the only time Edward speaks so harshly of the gay community or Following Shepard.

Castor has been awake, and still, for an hour. His wrists burn and his stomach hurts from hunger, and everywhere Edward is touching him is moist with sweat, but he can not bring himself to leave Edward's embrace. As near as he can tell, Edward is asleep — but he doesn't dare to turn for fear of breaking the spell.

16

Barb Kerzenmacher did not often come to meetings of the SGA. Two visits, in consecutive months, were nearly a record, and not one she hoped to break. The first visit was to stop a floor fight she knew was coming. The second one was to stop what she saw as an insurrection. Neither visit had the intended effect.

When Seth came to that same meeting, it actually was a personal record — it was the only meeting he ever attended. He entered, 30 minutes late, flanked and supported by two members of Following Shepard. He was gaunt and his eyes dark. They were trying to hide it, but he was clearly in need of the two men beside him to walk any real distance. His shirt was a red button down, wide and with flowing sleeves. It fit to his shoulders, but below the chest it hid everything.

The meeting wrapped up old business, and the next point on the agenda, called "Words from our Sponsor," was Barb's turn to speak. She stood. A bracelet of prayer beads slipped from under the cuff of her jacket and settled on her hand as she made the attempt. The beads matched the jacket in color, and were unblemished. They were obviously rarely worn. She was not quiet about the effort involved in standing. She read from a prepared statement.

"It has come to my attention that an unauthorized and unregistered student group has been meeting, calling themselves Following Shepard.

Students are reminded that only student groups recognized by the student senate are allowed the use of university resources. Students wh—"

"Or what?" Seth interrupted. Barb glared but read on.

"Students who post any unauthorized flyers on university property may be subject to disciplinary action. It is also important that we conduct ourselves in accordance with the rules, as our behavior reflects on the SGA."

Seth stood, of his own volition, but slowly. Drawn up to his full height, they were eye to eye and towered over those seated on the floor. His hand clasped where a leather book would have been. "That's an awfully vague threat, Barb."

Freshmen did not call Barb Kerzenmacher by her first name. She bristled. The expression on her face was not a pleasant one. "Exact disciplinary measures would depend on the record of the students involved, and can be up to and including expulsion."

Seth's laugh was cut short by a cough. "Either you're a terrible liar, or we're all paying thousands of dollars a year for the privilege of attending a university that expels its students for free speech and peaceful assembly."

"Free speech and assembly aren't regulated. The use of university resources is only available at the discretion of its officials."

"My friends and I don't use university resources. We meet at an off-campus location and provide everything ourselves."

"The locations where the flyers have been posted are university resources."

"Well,"

Seth laid a hand on a nearby chair and leaned in for support. There was little depression in the chair, though it carried a large portion of his weight. His two bearers made moves to support him, but he dismissed them with a glance.

"Well I don't know who's posting them. I'm not. Do you know who? And what does that have to do with your organization?"

"It's not hard to draw a line between these posters and the SGA."

"It is without proof. Because unless you know who's posting them, unless there's proof, the only thing they have in common is the word gay."

"There's membership overlap. Students involved in the SGA are also involved in your group."

Seth stood straight again. His lip turned to a smirk, and there was fire in his eyes.

"How do you know that? What evidence do you have that's true? My friends and I don't keep a roll, and at least I've been told, the attendance roll of your organization is private and confidential. It all comes back to, we're the gay groups. Or rather, I'm the gay group and you're the one sent to police us."

"I'm not here to police anyone. I'm here to support and protect the SGA."

Seth only took a single, small step towards Kerzenmacher, but the whole room felt the distance between them shrink. She did not step backwards. She did not move, except to flare her eyes and dig her thick brown shoes into the carpet.

"I can't imagine why anyone would. This organization is useless to gay students. Its adviser is a willing residence life watchdog, its president hopelessly incapable of understanding the cause, and its purpose to ease straight guilt and keep the proud and outspoken among us quiet and in line. Your social events are empty imitations of straight culture, your meetings are repetitive discussions of nothing worthwhile and above all, you don't approve of our true lifestyle. You think gay means living the straight and narrow life with a same-sex partner. We are so much more than that. And right now, we're leaving."

Seth turned, walked briskly and 12 other students left the meeting on the spot. One observant SGA member noticed that 10 of them wore matching choker necklaces with a pendant of red glass. Seth, Barney and Sawyer were the only exiting students without them. Barney and Sawyer arrived on their own, but they left with the group. The student also noticed that Seth grasped his head and leaned heavily on his bearers once back out on the porch.

The SGA meeting lasted another intensely awkward 20 minutes. Kerzenmacher offered a jumbled explanation of what she was trying to do, very little of it in complete sentences, and none of it exactly remembered by any attendees, Joann went through the motions of getting to the end of the meeting, and everyone else was deeply interested in not being there.

At the next SGA meeting, three people were in attendance — all of them straight. Following Shepard was up to 13 in regular attendance.

17

Only one of the five men surrounding Nathan Tanner outside the bar beats him. Four men stand by as Nathan is held against the bricks of the wall. One patron rushes by and stumbles down the street.

The sheer sleeves and chest patch on Nathan's t-shirt were torn in the bar. Only half an arm's length apart, Nathan and his attacker's breath form a single cloud of steam in the cold March air.

Nathan purses his lips at his attacker, and is dropped to the ground and clumsily kicked in the knee. The attacker manages to get another kick to his gut before Nathan curls up. The attacker's companions say nothing during the beating, or when he murmurs 'faggot' a few times, but pouring the remainder of his beer onto Nathan is apparently too much. The attacker shrugs the hands of his companions off his shoulders and drops the empty bottle onto Nathan. Beer and blood drip the short distance to the sidewalk. The police car pulling by doesn't turn on his siren, even for a single flash. No report is ever made of the incident.

Eirinn answers the door when Nathan arrives at the house. He is slumped against the wall and as Eirinn brings the boy in, his pain is such that Eirinn wonders how he had made it to their door. Once in the kitchen, Eirinn retrieves the first aid kit and begins to inspect his patient. Shallow cuts skirt the edges of his face. His nose has stopped bleeding. His lip is still going.

Eirinn dabs at the cuts with hydrogen peroxide and involuntary tears begin to carve streaks out of the dirt on Nathan's face. He flinches only once, but doesn't retreat from Eirinn's cotton swab. Neither does Eirinn retreat from Nathan's tight grasp on his knee. Nathan meets Eirinn's eyes, intense with care and focussed on the cuts, momentarily before staring intently at the McCam fridge door. But for the kitchen, the house is dark and the windows black with the night outside. The world is that room between the two of them, until Seth stumbles down the final step into the kitchen.

Eirinn nimbly spins around his chair and slides it under Seth, the peroxide soaked cotton still in his hand. Seth collapses into the chair. He looks through dulled eyes and his robe is untied. Eirinn is stern.

"You should be in bed."

"What happened?"

Seth's gaze bores into Nathan, though his speech is slurred and he can't sit precisely still. Nathan recounts the attack quickly, unable to look away. Eirinn bandages Nathan's face, but when he mentions the kicks to his gut, Eirinn lifts Nathan's shirt level to his chest. There is no room to recoil, but Nathan flinches. Eirinn does not apologize. He examines and prods with clinical precision. He does not, however, ask if it hurts.

Nathan's chest will be one big bruise by morning. The discoloration all the way across has already begun. Eirinn now commands Nathan's attention.

"You need to go to the hospital. There could be serious internal bleeding or damage to your vital organs."

Nathan looks away to the fridge again. Eirinn looks between them, tired of half-truths and insufficient information. There is palpable silence before Seth breaks it.

"He can't."

Eirinn's eyes demand an explanation from Nathan, but Seth gives it again.

"Too many questions will be asked. And it'll get back to his parents. And they'll want to know why it happened."

"You're risking your life."

67

"I'm doing that either way."

Nathan doesn't even manage to look Eirinn in the eye for the whole sentence.

Eirinn doesn't focus much on his classes the next day, but he goes. None of the members of Following Shepard do. They gather in the McCam living room.

"Never forget; they shed first blood."

The living room is full, but Nathan and Flip have the couch to themselves, Nathan laying out with his head in Flip's lap. Flip pets Nathan's hair, but carefully — there are few areas of Nathan's body that are safe to touch.

"Blood is our inheritance. Our forebears surrendered their blood at the hands of their fathers. Today we have surrendered blood at the hands of our enemies. Today we are brothers in blood, bathed in it, baptised in it. We bleed together. They will bleed alone."

The sermon Seth gives is written down in his book of them, but his vision from the night before, the third on record, wasn't in the book of dreams. It is faithfully recorded, however, in Jamie Boanerges's journal. It appears Seth recounted it only to him.

> He was on fire, made of fire, the ground beneath him scorched black at his feet. My shadow was in a circle at my own. He leapt forward and was upon me. He took me up into the sky and grasped me. I was enveloped in flames but did not burn. I did not resist. He threw me to the ground.
> I saw the relics then, floating above me and shining down. A club, of old wood, fire-hardened and turned at a lathe. A sling, of linen and stone. A band of iron to be clasped at the fist. These were weapons of war.
> A voice came into my mind. "By these signs you shall know your patron, and by these relics you might speak the word of your patron to your people. Bring the life of your patron to your people. Show the death of your patron to your people. Lay this sacrifice upon your

patron's altar, and then return to the Church, blessed among the acolytes. Do this to serve your Lord."

The local police tracked a series of savage beatings over the next month. Descriptions of the assailants varied, but there were always three attackers and three weapons: a scorched baseball bat, a sack full of rocks, and a tekko made out of rebar. Similar attacks were reported along the route Following Shepard took to Laramie. The weapons were never found.

18

The scene starts en media res in the McCam living room. Sawyer is moaning and there are 9 people on the screen having some sort of sex. After Barney returns from pressing record, there are 10. Nathan, Flip and Seth are missing from this video, but otherwise all of the members of Following Shepard are there, and none of them could be unaware of the camera.

———————————

Jamie Boanerges and Aras Fisher took each other's virginity on January 13, 1999. Jamie's journal is surprisingly physical in its description.

> "I have laid with a man, and he with me. I have never taken such pleasure in sin. His mouth upon mine, his flesh upon mine, our bodies on fire and alive. There were awkward moments and kisses with mashed faces but every touch of skin on skin echoed and danced across my nerves.
> It was the first time for both of us."

The film I am watching is date stamped — at the time of filming, Eirinn is at his parents' house for dinner, Nathan was recovering from his attack, and Seth was bedridden for two days. In fact, at the time they were upstairs. Nathan's absence on this video is noteworthy, as it is the only one he does not participate in.

The best description I've heard of the relationship of Nathan Tanner and Flip Bolani is that Flip was Nathan's favorite lap. The curve of his neck fit neatly over Flip's thigh, better than any other thigh he'd tried.

Out of all of the members of Following Shepard, Nathan appears to have had the most sexual partners by an order of magnitude. His high school disciplinary records are sealed to the public, but three different students report catching him in the act during school — including one who caught the other. His teacher, another who caught him in the act, describes him as a C student.

"I'd like to say he'd have done better if he only tried, but there was never even any evidence of that."

Nathan's parents each drive Porsches and their house has multiple wings. The Tanner family wealth dates back two generations — his parents work, but they've never actually needed the money.

At 16, Flip Bolani attempted to kill himself with a triple dose of maximum strength tylenol. He managed to write about a third of a note before beginning to vomit non-stop and being rushed to the emergency room by his parents. He was diagnosed with clinical depression two weeks later. He wasn't prescribed antidepressants until almost a year later, and while the prescription was fulfilled, the full bottle was discovered amongst his belongings in his dorm room along with two others from other psychiatrists along the way. There's no evidence he ever took a single pill.

Bolani is described as withdrawn by those who can describe him at all. He doesn't appear to have ever attended any of the clubbing outings, and by the time of the Laramie trip, was failing the majority of his classes by lack of attendance. Once the members started staying at the McCam house full time, Flip Bolani almost never left. He's only ever seen with Tanner or alone. Their relationship isn't exclusive, at least for Tanner.

There's a lot going on in the video. Jamie Boanerges and Aras Fisher are paired off on their own for the whole time, and they spend a great deal of time out of frame. Boanerges is surprisingly loud. Even when he is not in frame, the rhythm of their activities is still quite apparent. At one point, about 15 minutes in, they return to frame and Boanerges is on top of Fisher while kissing Barney Joseph.

Over the course of the hour long video, Jamie Miner is on the receiving end of nearly every partner in the room. At one point, a four way daisy chain is attempted, but they're never quite able to get a rhythm down.

The others occasionally break off into pairs, but they're irregular and inconsistent.

The relationship between Barney Joseph and Sawyer Kana is more conventional — they go out on dates, share activities together, even plan to move in together the following year. They just, while being boyfriends, sleep with other people. It is a casual definition not regarded as abnormal by the gay students I talk to — in fact they refer to Joseph and Kana's relationship as the healthiest of any gay students at JU. Both are out of the closet, emotionally well adjusted and doing well in school.

There's no one person in command of everyone, and at certain points, it looks so much like a cluster of writhing bodies that it's hard to tell whose arm belongs to whom.

Edward and Sean, after climaxing, withdraw to watch. Edward even leaves, only to return with a drink for himself and Sean, who rejoins after a few minutes, beer still in hand.

On the third watch, pieces of a fascinating command structure begin to appear. There aren't a great deal of words spoken, but clear instructions emerge out of facial cues and bodily rhythms. Arthur only acts at Andi's insistence. Nobody tells Edward what to do. Barney and Sawyer watch each other, often, but are otherwise free agents. Jamie Miner doesn't kiss on the mouth, and Sean looks at the camera a lot.

Sean Davidson and Jamie Miner are in a relationship nobody describes as healthy. Some don't even describe it as consensual. Miner is consistently seen with bruises. He never joins the group without Davidson, and when he's there, he looks to Davidson before making any decision. They do participate in sex outside the two of them, but only together.

After the last of them have finished, Barney also turns off the camera. He smiles as it shuts off. The video is pornography; not so different than any video available for purchase. Yet somehow, presented without argument or justification, without plot or explanation, each successive scene feels more like a sermon on sexual mores from all the members of Following Shepard.

19

I'm told a little over 1,000 students attend here. I still can't get over how high schools, even ones that weren't my own, seem so much smaller now.

On the door to the classroom, there's a 3 inch rainbow sticker, surrounded by old scratch marks. The sticker on top is fresh, but the adhesion is uneven from all the gashes underneath. It's been removed several times by pen and fingernail. On the door window, covering it completely, is a handwritten paper sign: GLSEN meeting. The teacher meets me outside the door. She is a small woman with a wide smile. She is at least 40 but moves like 24, and assures me she was almost a dancer. As she grasps the door knob with one hand, she takes my wrist with the other.

"I protect these children, Mr. Tabari. More than their mothers and fathers. Mind that."

Her smile returns before she opens the door and introduces me.

The classroom inside is ill-fitted to the surrounding school. Sheer, glittering fabric bunting hangs about the room. The cinder-block walls are only visible in three spots, and the windows have their own hazy curtains. The cloth looks new, but there is dust on top. It is a permanent fixture of the room.

I'd hazard a guess that nearly every student in the school with neon hair is in this room. There are 16 students, and only 5 have hair that's not dyed. A couple boys wear tight fitted clothing, and are dangerously skinny to boot. One chubby boy wears an old t-shirt he's swimming in. There's bruising, old and new, on two of the students. It peeks out of one boy's multi-colored knit armsleeves. I have agreed not to ask what they are from.

This meeting was arranged a month in advance. It took two one-hour phone calls and one 5 minute meeting to get permission. The calls were filled with questions, about my work and about me. On meeting in person, Ms. Moore mostly shook my hand and stared into my eyes, then spelled out the conditions of my presence. This group keeps no roll; and I have agreed to respect individual anonymity. The students have been told not to give me their names, and I have agreed not to ask for them. In the words of Ms. Moore, "if the parents of my students should read your work, they should not recognize their own children." Out of respect for both the students and their anonymity, I have not changed any of the details of the students or the meeting. There is, however, insufficient timely information to identify any Moore High students.

Groups like these, sometimes called chapters of GLSEN (Gay Lesbian Straight Education Network) or GSA (Gay Straight Alliance) have widely expanded since the first ones were formed in the late 80s, but not without resistance. One group at East High School in Salt Lake City was so opposed that the school board banned all non-academic groups from meeting, just to ensure the GSA could not meet. For all the efforts and resistance, groups only exist in a handul of schools per district. Statistics in this area are difficult. Many groups, like the one at this Lima high school, are unregistered even with their own schools, let alone any national organization. And all of them have strict policies about anonymity, so an accurate count of members is impossible. Many in rural areas follow a similar parallel — an adamant teacher whose passion will not brook obstruction or local politics.

It's two weeks before the end of school. For many of the Seniors, that means escape and emancipation. Three boys, who haven't attended a meeting in months, have come to find out what happened to Barney and

Sawyer. One blue-haired girl will brook no insult to their character, and accuses me of lying several times. All of them have more questions than answers. The little information they have has been scraped from national news coverage. One student obtained a copy of the JU article, but it only confirmed the names of the victims for them.

Barney and Sawyer visited the group a dozen times over the course of the school year. They attended four meetings, took the group on 3 short outings, and one day long trip to the Short North, a gay district in Columbus. Four times, including their last visit only two weeks before leaving for Laramie, the pair arranged for Somewhere in Time to open up their dance floor on a Saturday afternoon and brought along several members of Following Shepard. On the third such outing, Sawyer and Jamie Miner performed in drag.

There's no evidence of untoward behavior between the members of Following Shepard and the students. No alcohol was ever served at the events, the high school students even drove each other home. Several of the students have obvious crushes, especially the blue haired girl and one of the absentee boys. While it's plausible to believe they'd keep such information from a journalist, the boys are quite frank about their sexual activity with older men. I look to the teacher after these answers and my silent question is met with daring glare.

I can not harmonize the two pictures of Barney and Sawyer. I can not conceive of a person so grounded that they would lighten the burdens of 16 teenagers isolated even from their families, yet end up in such a terrible position themselves. Neither come from a broken home. Sawyer's parents don't approve of homosexuality, but it doesn't seem to have tarnished their feelings toward him, and they recognize his life choices as his to make. I have such an incomplete picture of both of them.

There are disagreements and infighting that pop up during the meeting — but their sense of community is clear. Few students have many friends outside this room. Many are not allowed to be themselves. To them, Barney and Sawyer, are older, but they are not outsiders. These kids have dealt with abuse I can only imagine. And to each of them, graduation is escape — most to another city, never to return again. But death is new. They do not know what to do with it.

As I leave the room, one Sophomore chases after me. In the first 15 minutes of the meeting, citing fearlessness in the face of oppression, but staring defiantly at Ms. Moore the whole time, he started the conversation about Barney and Sawyer, and prefaced it with his name. Of all the students in the room, he is the only one whose impression of me seems to have noticeably changed. The distrust from my arrival was still around for my departure; even to the end, the blue-haired girl tried to prevent other students from sharing any negative opinions of Barney and Sawyer. The Sophomore is different; he's said little about Barney and Sawyer besides his opening salvo, and I noticed several times during the meeting when he was staring at me.

I stop, and he catches up to me — he touches my hand, and it's gentle.

"This is a safe space," he says. "For everyone. If you ever need someone to open up to, we're here. We're harsh sometimes, but we're here."

My own desire to tell him I'm not gay seems offensive at that moment. I also am certain it would fall on deaf ears.

20

In the 2 weeks leading up to the Laramie trip, Seth only leaves the house twice. It is, by this point, mathematically impossible for him to avoid failing out of JU. He hasn't handed in an assignment this month or even attended an exam.

Eirinn attends his classes during this time, but is failing himself because virtually the only thing he does outside of class is tend to Seth's needs, which are constant. He vomits unexpectedly, and sometimes without waking. He sleeps constantly, except when his headaches are bad enough to wake him. His speech is slurred, but what words he has are used to refuse being taken to the hospital.

There are two good days in this time, and only one Eirinn knows about. The members of Following Shepard are constantly present, and though Andi frequently asks after his condition, it is Arthur who shares the burden of Seth's care. The others, at Seth's request and Andi's insistence are largely unaware, though Eirinn sees Edward Argent occupy a familiar spot outside the bedroom.

At the age of 11, Seth McCam got the chicken pox and almost immediately gave it to Eirinn. At the time, Eirinn's parents were unable to take time off — Dillon was in school and at work, and Meara's two jobs did not afford her a great deal of overlapping paid time off.

Eirinn spent the two weeks of his infection at the McCam house. Katelyn McCam, who was acutely vulnerable to shingles, spent the two weeks on a business trip. Matthew took the time off to spend with the boys.

He kept them in soup and blankets, but other than the occasional admonishment not to scratch, he largely left the boys alone with the TV in Seth's room.

Matthew McCam only ever bought a handful of toys for Seth. Seth only ever saw him buy one, a dark brown teddy bear. It was instantly his favorite, which Katelyn tried to pretend didn't upset her.

Its nose is hard and plastic, and was always cold unless Seth had been holding it for a few hours. The pads of his feet are the same material, but never seem to be as cold. The shag of the plush material is deep and faded but surprisingly unworn.

The bear sat between them during their illness. Matthew's arrival was always heralded by a creaking floorboard outside Seth's bedroom door, and whenever his father was about to enter the room, Seth would shove it into Eirinn's arms, but take it back when his father was out of sight. Eirinn was just happy to be part of the game. Years later, he realized that the creaking spot in the hallway floor is more worn than the whole rest of the hallway, from years of use; and standing there, even with the door open only a crack, you can see all of Seth's bed.

After the first few days of their convalescence, the bear just sat between them on the bed, lightly compressed as Seth leaned over to Eirinn and they fast-forwarded through the commercials of a VHS tape of Teenage Mutant Ninja Turtles. They napped and slept often, and reluctantly did the homework that was brought home, but they spent every moment together.

Eirinn wouldn't describe his feelings towards that week as shameful, but he certainly knew better than to speak about it, even to Seth. He does not track the evolution of a romantic relationship between them. Certainly at that age, romance was still developmentally a few years off, but Eirinn speaks of the memories with a specific kind of fondness that is not hard to recognize.

March 27, 1999 is one of Seth's good days. His headaches are gone, and light no longer sets them off. He walks on his own, eats solid food and moreover keeps it down. For the first time in a month, Eirinn goes to bed before Seth. When he wakes the next morning, the house is empty. The long-term houseguests are all gone, but so is Seth. On the nightstand is a Hi-8 video tape, Seth's three journals and Edward Argent's, with the Following Shepard flyer folded between the glass cover and the first page. Seth's dream journal is bookmarked to its penultimate entry, and on the bookmark was written 12/25/1998 in Argent's hand. The writing is shakier than any other entry, and dirt is smudged on the page.

FIRST VISION

I am in the Cathedral, but it is empty. The air feels like fall. Light is coming through the rose window behind the altar. The altar is blue. The altar has no clothes on it, only a glass cup of red wine. I must reach that cup. I walk towards it but it does not get closer. I run, but I make no progress. I jump and fly, but the altar does not get any closer. Someone is behind me. They say: "You will not reach it."

When I turn I see no one, but a light comes from the baptismal font. I walk to it. The inside has no bottom. From the depths, a woman rises. She looks like my mom, except for her six wings. Two cover her face, two her feet and two are outstretched.

"The clarion voice of the Almighty God bears a message to you, son of Matthew. Be not afraid."

Her voice shakes the walls. I fall to my knees.

"The father of the Church names you base ill, son of Matthew. He declares you unfit to be the lowest of his acolytes, and would deny you the very body of Christ. Leave the Church. As of this day, you have no Church. Seek faith anew."

I feel tears down my face, though I did not feel them leave my eyes.

"Seek a new patron, and know your patron by this: He bears the name of the father. He is struck down by those who offer hospitality. His death brings forth the angels."

I cannot look at her.

21

On April 1, 1999, HR 1082 of the 106th Congress, known as the Hate Crimes Prevention Act, went to a floor vote. The SGA had planned a field trip to join a rally on the mall over their spring break. The SGA was one of about 30 school groups who came to show support. All told, less than 6 months after Matthew Shepard's death 206 students showed up to support the legislation spawned by it. Had the students of Following Shepard been with them, the JU SGA would have represented the largest delegation. Aside from a University of Wyoming delegation, they travelled the farthest. Without the students in Following Shepard, there were five people from JU — including Barb Kerzenmacher, and not including Joann Bianchi.

Lee Prince is one of the JU students who attended the rally. He has a surfer's blonde mop, intense blue eyes and a manner several people describe as off-putting, but our interview ends up mostly one-sided in the wrong direction. He only ever attended a handful of SGA meetings — I only need to talk to him about the rally. But half an hour later, he knows more than I've told my advisor about the story. We do manage to get around to what I need eventually.

"206 students sounds impressive until you put them on the National Mall. We didn't occupy one-eighth of the place. We didn't stretch beyond the steps to the hill. It was 15 degrees and we huddled. We were prepared for the weather, or the temperature at least. The Wyoming students were even prepared for the wind."

His manner shifts as he tells a story instead of hearing it. His sentences are full of pauses and he sounds like a third of the way to a Christopher Walken impression. The off-putting thing starts to make sense.

"It was a fantastic disappointing experience. I mean, this is a national cause — a national rally and kids are dying. And 206 people showed up. There are millions of students across the country in undergrad. If one one-hundredth of one percent showed up, it would have been 10 times the number of people there."

He's quoting statistics from an anonymous letter to the editor that ran in The Light two weeks after the rally. It was the last issue of the 1998-99 school year.

"But… there were so many people to meet, and talk to. It was like taking all of the most passionate people from schools all over the East coast and putting them in one room. It was amazing. I met a straight girl who told her parents she was a lesbian just to prove they'd be upset about it. I met a guy who came out in high school by hijacking the morning announcements."

The JU task force assigned to track the use of university resources established a rough timeline of the events starting March 28, 1999, when the SGA left Ohio bound for DC, the 13 members of Following Shepard among them. The trip from campus to DC took about 6 hours. There wasn't enough money for university sponsored transportation, so the students carpooled in a caravan of 7 cars.

The caravan arrived at a hotel near the Franconia-Springfield station at 6:35 p.m. At 6:40 p.m., Barb Kerzenmacher distributed the per diem for the trip — $20 per day, working out to $100 per person and $1200 in total to the members of Following Shepard. Seth, not having registered for the trip, did not receive a per diem.

The students were allowed a choice of restaurants — Kerzenmacher went to the Bob Evans across the street. When she returned, 4 of the student cars were gone. They belonged to Edward Argent, Sawyer Kana, Arthur Pascal and Aras Fisher. Kerzenmacher, immediately suspicious, took a roll call of the students. With so many still at dinner, the process took nearly an hour, before she could confirm that the 12 registered students had left. She immediately informed the director of residence life, who in turn informed the parents of each student involved, with the exception of Edward Argent and Andi Patras, neither of whom had parents on their emergency contact information. The office of residence life received over 150 calls and emails that night. Of the 10 students with parents contacted, the parents of Sawyer Kana were the only ones aware of the trip — six of the sets of parents weren't aware their sons were gay, and one stopped calling after that become apparent.

The task force came to the conclusion that no university rules had been broken, and procedures were properly followed by the faculty and staff members involved. All students were 18 or older, so no special permission was required to attend, and the funds had been obtained and distributed in a manner consistent with other student group trips. Had they returned from the trip, all 12 students would have faced a hearing most likely resulting in punishments from probation to expulsion for theft of university property.

After leaving DC, the students also left the scope of the university inquiry. Their trail is fuzzy the first night. Probability and timing indicate that they probably stopped for the night of March 28 somewhere along I-70 or I-68 in Maryland, but there's no certainty as to the exact location. It seems likely that they paid out of the cash per diem they were all given.

On March 29, at 11:17 a.m., two stained glass windows of St. Nicholas church in Zanesville Ohio were hit with pink spray paint cans and then shattered by bricks. The church was offering a reconciliation mass. By the time the first eye witness made it outside, they only heard the car that had already peeled around the corner. Two large pink triangles had been painted on the church's front doors. At 11:18, Seth McCam's credit card paid for a diner meal for 11 people about a half mile away.

22

By the night of March 29, the Following Shepard caravan made it as far as Champaign, Illinois. Seth's credit card was used shortly after midnight to pay for two rooms at the motel on the edge of town.

Three hours earlier, 5 men were individually attacked, each shortly after exiting a separate Dayton bar, and each by a gang of 10-12 young men. They were grabbed from the street, pulled into an alley and beaten, and then held down as a pink triangle was spray painted onto their faces. Much of the holding was done by Sean Davidson, and the spraying by Jamie Miner.

Davidson and Miner met during Miner's first week at JU; like Seth McCam, he is a Freshman. Davidson is a Senior, and Miner is his first boyfriend in quite some time. In his own Freshman year, he earned a reputation for being too aggressive with his lovers. In his Sophomore year he hit one, outside the bedroom, and since then his reputation preceded him and kept him from further entanglements until he met Jamie.

After the attacks, each victim visited the hospital emergency room, two were admitted for eye injury. None were sent to intensive care, but all of them have permanent scars from the wounds dealt that night. The bartenders of each location were interrogated for the police reports, but need little help recalling the incident 6 months later when I interview them.

They describe a group of 8-12 boys, coming in to a mostly empty bar (it being Monday night) in varying levels of rowdiness. The bartenders use different verbage, and describe it with varying levels of offense, but some version of a sneer and "those boys were all over each other" makes it into each story. They were asked to leave all but one of the bars, the last of which only had two other patrons. In each case. the victim muttered or said a homophobic remark before leaving, and was shortly followed by the boys who fled the scene after each beating and proceeded to another bar.

The entire spree took place within the span of 3 hours. Aras Fisher spent the majority of that time driving the lead car, and Seth spent it in and out of consciousness in the back seat. Neither had any alcohol, but all the others did.

Barney Joseph and Sawyer Kana came out of each bar first, and the most intoxicated. At three of the bars, they followed the eventual victim. At the other two, the victim followed them as they held hands and kissed out the door. Whatever the intent of each patron might have been in leaving the bar, whether to leave or attack the bait couple, none of the victims were given time to express it before Nathan Tanner, Flip Bolani, Sean Davidson and Jamie Miner attacked. There was some change up between fists and weapons, except for Davidson who apparently always used the rebar tekko.

Davidson and Miner grew up no strangers to domestic violence. Both suffered at the hands of abusive fathers. Miner's mother died in childbirth, and those who know the family say that his father never got over it, and that Jamie's behavior exacerbated the issue. Miner did not do well in school, and was both highly sexually active and bad at hiding it, until his Senior year in high school, when his father threatened to throw him out.

Davidson's father never stopped beating his family — until his son stopped him. When he was 15, Sean's sister, after a particularly violent outburst, drove away crying and angry — and was killed in an accident less than 20 minutes later. When Sean found out, he fought with his father, and won. He beat his father so severely he was hospitalized for two days. The tables never turned back. Matthew once bragged to a lover that for the last two years he lived at home, his father lived in fear.

For both of them, abuse turned out to be an inescapable cycle. Miner was frequently seen with bruises he could never adequately explain away. There is no record of the abuse in any of the journals of those in Following Shepard. It seems impossible that they should not have noticed it; the abusive relationship seems to be common knowledge for the entire JU gay community. Or rather, the community such as it was after April 4, the events of which effectively shrunk it by half. None of the students seem blind to the abuse, but none know what to do about it, either. Miner's sexuality isn't a known fact all across campus — and involving authority figures would necessarily involve spreading that information, likely back to his father, who would remove him from school or worse if he heard that his sexual activity was continuing. Inaction seemed the best choice.

On March 30, the group traveled to Lincoln, Nebraska. Seth's credit card was used to check in at a motel on the west edge of town, this time in the late afternoon. Aras and Seth remained in the room that night when the rest went out. No police reports from that night seem to be linked to their journey. But the attacks did continue, and these victims fought back.

Upon their return, the four attackers from the previous night had multiple contusions and cuts — and not a small amount of pink paint on them. Edward Argent, nodding to Aras, humorlessly said "You should see the other guys."

The attacks did not continue the next night in Cheyenne. Edward Argent went to a liquor store and bought an excessive amount of alcohol. Aras heard them partying while he tended to Seth in the next room. Seth left the bed to vomit 4 times with Aras' help. After the fourth time, Arthur Pascal and Andi Patras entered the room. Aras was urged to leave.

When they woke the next morning, Aras had gone and taken his car with him. The remaining twelve continued on to Laramie.

23

The 12 final members of Following Shepard sit in a circle, Seth against the fencepost. Andi Patras is at his left hand, Arthur Pascal returned to his right after starting the camera. From its tripod, the camera sees 8 of them, Andi at the center. Sean, Sawyer, Barney and Castor are not within the range of the lens.

It would have been 40 degrees out there during the ceremony.

They are all dressed in loose white shirts, and their faces are pale from the cold and wind.

Andi makes no effort to hide the drugs he withdraws from behind him. The plastic bag passed around the circle contains one less small packet with each set of hands it passes through. The white salt in each packet is Phencyclidine, and it is taken,snorted, without ceremony. Their comfort is immediately and visibly improved.

As they grow red faced, each of the members stops shivering as well.

Seth begins to speak.

> "We are here. We have journeyed to the end of our patron's waking life. Here he was taken, here he was beaten, and here he wept until falling from consciousness for the last time. We sit on the ground consecrated by his blood. We sit on the ground washed by his tears. He died of their sins. He died for our sins."

Andi withdraws a large, heavy glass from a bag and fills it with wine. He passes it around, and each member takes a sip.

> "This post was the place of his crucifixion. This post is where we have been led. In the world, we have been hardened by fire. In our home, we were joined by flesh. Here we will become one family, by blood. Here we will form a covenant of brothers; of ourselves and to ourselves, to replace the one we are denied by our fathers."

As the wine glass completes the round and comes to Seth, he takes a sip, and pauses.

> "I have no more tears...
> What else have I to shed?"

Seth's speech becomes lightly slurred. Around the circle, everyone visible, except Andi, becomes restless. Andi stands. He takes the wine glass from Seth and sets it on top of the post. Seth's eyes are closed as Andi kicks him in the gut — but no exclamation or look of surprise appears. The attack was planned, rehearsed. And it is repeated.

Arthur is next, and after him, one by one the boys around the circle stand, deliver a blow to Seth, and return to their seats. Cuts appear at his face starting with the third kick. Droplets of blood from his wounds and wine from the glass spray to the post behind him as his head is struck into it. It is absorbed like rain.

Edward delivers the last blow and takes the wine glass from the post. He finishes it, and then returns to his seat. Seth resumes his speech.

> "I shed my clothes after yet before you,
> That my body might be whole for your blessing.

Seth disrobes. Despite their thin veil, the robes hide a great deal. In every photo in the McCam house, Seth is chubby — 5'11", often weighing in at around 180 lbs. In the video, his ribcage is nearly visible. The skin is angry and red in several places, more than one in the distinct shape of the feet and fists that just struck him.

Once he is naked, all of the members follow suit — simultaneously this time, not waiting for the last one to complete before beginning. When they are seated again, he continues.

> "I shed my blood after yet before you,
> That through this glass I may see your Light."

Taking the now empty glass in both hands, he breaks the stem in half. Andi holds the glass half as Seth drags the now sharp edge of the stem across the wrist of his outstretched arm, and bleeds over the stem and into the glass. It turns dark with the blood, almost black on the video.

He passes the glass to the left, and the ritual is repeated, in turn, by each of the members, until the full round is made. Not everyone cuts as cleanly or makes such a small incision.

> "I take of the blood of my brothers,
> where you stood and where you fell,
> that I may follow on your path."

Seth drinks from the glass and passes it to the left again. It does not make the full rounds before the members begin to collapse onto the ground. Arthur tries to embrace Andi Patras, who pushes him away. Arthur tries to put his pants on, gets them over his ankles, and climbs the fence. He lands on the other side of the post, legs bound to the top and arms splayed out behind him. Patras collapses, arms and legs outstretched in an X.

The members of Following Shepard died of a variety of causes, but the coroner's report indicated that it was ultimately a race to see which of the fatal items they encountered would take them first. Four had lethal doses of PCP, but of those one died of hypothermia. Three had cut along an artery with the glass and died of blood loss. All 12 had small amounts of cyanide in their systems, but only Argent received a fatal dose — investigators were not able to determine how. Two of the members who might have survived the PCP and blood loss also succumbed to hypothermia. In the end, it is Jamie Boanerges who saves Seth's life.

Most of the members break off into their most common pairs. Edward and Castor, Barney and Sawyer, Flip and Nathan, Jamie Miner and Sean all die in each other's arms. But with Aras gone, Jamie Boanerges embraces McCam, and wraps the loose shirts around them both. The doctors say the body heat and even minor protection from the wind are what kept McCam alive long enough to be found and revived.

24

The final entry in Seth's leather bound book is a forgery. With most of the sermons, there's evidence the words were delivered at some point, but not the last one. The rhetoric is a match, the letter shapes are convincing enough, but there are hesitation marks, about two to every word. The real author had to stop — consider how the next letter was made, possibly check against a reference.

The entry isn't long, but with all the hesitation marks it would have taken considerable time to inscribe into the book. The author's forgery skill is not expert, but not for lack of care. Despite the hesitations, there are no false starts or incorrect marks. There are no pages missing from the book, either. He may have practiced elsewhere, but inside the book, he got it on the first try.

> The angel was a lie: Abraham failed. Isaac was always meant to be sacrificed. Each of us, all of us is meant to be sacrificed. We were given God's greatest gift of life precisely to see if we could give it back. Each day we draw breath is a failure at God.
> We claw away from our fathers as they ran from theirs. But each of us opens our eyes and we are at the altar, on the altar. The torch is lit and the knife poised above our hearts. God has provided the lamb. Where our fathers faltered we will not. Moriah is our destiny. We will travel to the summit and none shall turn the resolve from our hearts, or the knife from our hands.

All of the members of Following Shepard, and Eirinn, had access to the journal. All the entries are undated, so a precise timeline is impossible, but given the delivery of the penultimate entry, it must have been written within the last week the members were still at JU.

Somewhere between Sunday, January 10, 1999 and Wednesday, January 13, Andi Patras met Seth McCam. Only Seth's word remains on when and what happened, and at the interview, his memory is uneven.

Seth awoke from his first coma on April 5, three days after the ceremony in Laramie. Against the advice of his doctors, he appeared at a press conference. On the same spot where Matthew Shepard's doctor had stood, less than six months prior, and announced that Matthew Shepard was dead, Seth stood to offer a statement to the press. Most of the reporters overlapped, as well.

The rock that sailed through the air and struck Seth in the temple that morning did not kill him. It was a factor, however, in the three day coma that followed. It was also a factor in the decision to get an MRI of Seth's head. Rather than the damage they expected to find, the doctors found a very large tumor deep in Seth's brain that had been there, they suspected, a very long time.

The drugs present at the ceremony were purchased by Arthur Pascal. The robes by Sawyer Kana. The alcohol was provided by Edward Argent. The lead car was driven by Barney Joseph. The plan, however, appears to have been provided by Andi Patras.

It's unclear how many of the other members of Following Shepard knew what they were getting into. The violence along the route turned Aras Fisher away, but he was the only one who stopped.

The wounds that caused their deaths were deemed self-inflicted by the coroner. But they also had significant amounts of PCP in their systems, sufficient enough that they at least didn't feel what they were doing — possibly were totally unaware. Patras is no exception — he had the lowest dose, but still more than enough to feel the symptoms.

The Hi-8 tape left in the video camera at Laramie was full all the way from beginning to end. The Hi-8 tape left with Seth's journals is blank almost all the way to the end. The last five minutes are a video that I'm told the quality indicates was copied there. It's a video of Andi Patras, alone in the room, and addressing the camera directly. It's one he apparently tried to erase, unaware that he failed.

That day I stopped trying to convince people. Every person who tells me they don't believe in gay marriage? Pop. A little clock appears above their head, and it starts counting down until they die.
We're not winning, we've already won. We're just dragging out the fight because this endless war has made us patient and you need to pay. You burned us for 4,000 years and now we're gonna take it out of you in blood and loss and time. We're the tide coming in. The more you struggle, the more you hate us, the more people you'll show we're on the side of the angels, and we're coming to save your children.
You look at the numbers, you see — the future of the generations belong to us. You can hate us, but your children don't. And their children won't. And their children will be us. You're a ticking clock to already dead, the racist grandpa nobody even wants to visit. And even if their guilt compels them to come to your rest home where gay nurses and women doctors keep your body alive after your mind's gone sour, even if you're surrounded by family you'll be alone. You won't remember who they are and they'll be ashamed of you. And as quick as they can they'll forget you.
Your bloodline will live. But you'll be dead and forgotten and your way of life will be a stain on history.
12 of us are going to die, by our own hands on a Laramie hill. And every single one of us will be hailed a victim of your oppression. I don't think there's life after death for me, but I know the world I'm making for you is my heaven.
So join us. And die.

25

At the hospital, Eirinn claims to be Seth's older brother, and the only family Seth has. He does it without blinking as though it is expected and habit, and in truth it is the only reason they let us in to visit or tell us anything at all. The nurse we met first is slight in appearance; with short, dark, but greying hair. Her voice is deep, and has gravel to it, but a pervading warmth she does not attempt to hide. She tells us he is currently in recovery and can't be seen, with unexpected kindness.

On our drive, I had wondered what I would see in Eirinn when the two were reunited. Eirinn and I spent a five day road trip together, averaging 12 hours a day in the car. I had assumed his rare moments of emotion were slips in a mask; one I saw many subjects put on when speaking to a reporter.

In other rooms, I see reunited lovers quietly cry. I see some asleep aside their own comatose partners, and others laughing in defiance of the bad news they've just received. Eirinn is blank. He tends to Seth's needs with diligence. The calm I see on his face at Seth's bedside, the same calm I saw on his face at the fencepost, no longer seems a mask to me. He smiles with earnest thanks to the staff who come to check in. The smile disappears when they do, but its presence wasn't a lie. He feels the emotion and sets it aside. There are more important matters to tend to.

The nurses know we're sleeping in the car; we've nearly run out of money. When the nurse from the previous night comes back for a morning shift, she wakes us with a knock on the window and a cup of coffee for Eirinn. As we exit the car to follow her, she slides a staff parking tag on the dash. She brings us to the staff locker room and allows us to shower. I am surprised at her certainty; she doesn't look over her shoulder when letting us in.

I feel profoundly vulnerable, naked in the shower. The tiles are cold and uncomfortable, and the open air of the stalls allows a breeze everywhere. I can not help but jump everytime the door opens. The feeling of cleanliness also disappears the moment I put on the same dirty clothes. Eirinn trades his for ill-fitting, borrowed scrubs.

Helping us in, letting us use the shower — it must be against the rules; but the nurse doesn't seem to care. Eirinn expresses gratitude for the kindness. I don't know how to react. Hospitals are as alien to me as I imagine they are to most people, and I find myself frequently staring towards the outside.

An angry rain comes and goes throughout the day, which is not unusual for Wyoming. The clouds' stillness, however, is unusual. Through the window, they appear an unending mass across the sky. A breeze occasionally flexed the screens on the window and ensured the stone walls of the hospital were steadily drenched, but Wyoming's usual gales don't make their presence known during our stay at the hospital.

Outside of Seth's room, I'm out of place and always seem to be in someone's way. Eirinn easily knows his way around; it's like he's a stagehand in a theatre where he's worked for years. Eirinn told me he volunteered at the hospital where his mother worked, but I had the impression it had been a few sessions after school. That impression was clearly wrong. He knows what to expect; when Seth moves involuntarily, he doesn't jump as though the boy is waking up. When the machines falter or change, it's expected. But his eyes don't leave the bed as he tells me more about the trip to Ireland.

"He wasn't ill the first few days. And for the first time he wasn't scared of being seen. Ireland wasn't the most welcoming place. Outside of the right neighborhoods of Dublin it could get dangerous, but Seth didn't care. I think he only ever cared if his father found out, and on that trip, it was no longer a risk. The space between us vanished and the fear with it. We held hands."

His face changes. He smiles, and it's genuine and beautiful. It is a rare happy memory. We allow it to linger for a few minutes. The power of the simple gesture on his memory surprises me. For straight couples, holding hands in public stops being a major threshold to cross somewhere late in middle school. For Eirinn, it's not something he was sure he'd ever get. It was an offhand remark, describing something clearly not that casual.

In Ireland, Eirinn and Seth had the worst night of their life together. Seth, raving and incapacitated; Eirinn terrified and both of them 1000 miles from home. On our first day on the road, Eirinn told me of the night. The details of the rest of the trip waited until Eirinn was standing over the hospital bed, stroking Seth's hair. Before that night, they were in Ireland three days. It was cold, and it got dark early, but that hardly stopped the patrons of The George, Ireland's largest gay bar.

Tears come to Eirinn's eyes. As he talks about The George, he takes and strokes Seth's hand.

"Even then, The George dwarfed any gay bars we had ever been to. It's a palace. It's three stories tall. It was already nearly 15 years old during our visit, with a stage, two separate bars and a lounge. It's the center of Dublin's gay culture, the center of gay culture for an entire nation that legalized homosexual sex 6 years prior; which America hasn't done. And still, the first floor windows are blocked out against prying eyes."

A nurse shuffles in and Eirinn's happy memory of their relationship sinks back amongst the rest.

26

The sun is setting, but the windows of the hospital face East; so the only light on his face as he returns to the waking world is cold blue and silver, harsh and fluorescent. The sheet over Seth shifts and Eirinn checks the machines. Seth awoke from his coma on April 8, 1999.

It's small, involuntary movements at first. Shifts in breathing, twitches of the eye. Waking from a coma is nothing like movies or TV, and it's easy to see why. It would be terrible, slow and heartbreaking to watch. Coma survivors describe it from the inside like emerging into a patchwork reality. Their memories are disconnected as their senses and nerves come back online and muscles start to work again.

From the outside, it is hours of uncontrolled movements and slurred speech. Seth recovered remarkably quickly, we were told, even for a coma only lasting three days. When Seth reaches up and touches Eirinn's face, and then his chest, with two fingers, Eirinn finally cries. The doctor's see it as motor function progress, but Eirinn claims it's proof that Seth recognizes him. It's another four hours before Seth begins to speak.

This time is the clearest illustration I can imagine of how Eirinn is not like anyone else I have ever met. Seth is not wholly aware of himself or the situation as he recovers, but to Eirinn, or at least if it were anyone but Eirinn, this must be torture. He hasn't seen the love of his life in over a week — during which time Seth has been in two separate comas, and

Eirinn learned that he was running what the media is calling a cult out of their home, somehow in secret. Yet for four hours, Seth medically can't answer any questions. I would be enraged. Everyone I know would be enraged. Eirinn is not. At least, not here.

When, finally, Seth is able to speak, Eirinn does begin to ask questions. Out of necessity, the first ones are practical and immediate — both to aid in the recovery, and because higher reasoning is the last thing to return.

Seth is awake for 14 hours before Eirinn finally asks, "Why?"

Seth's smile is lopsided as he says "It seemed like a good idea at the time."

I'm sitting behind him, but judging from Seth's reaction, Eirinn's face contorts into one even Seth has never seen before.

"You don't get to make jokes today. You don't get to do that. Do you know what you've done?"

"I do."

"Is that all you have to say?"

"That's all you asked."

"This isn't an interrogation, Seth. Since when do you keep secrets from me?"

"Since they hurt you. I had to keep you out of this."

"You don't — you can't do that. You can't cut me out of your life. What did you think would happen? Did you think you could just leave me behind?"

"It wasn't safe, where I was going. I wanted you safe."

Eirinn stopped for a second. I heard a long, measured breath. The first question I had, and the one he had avoided thinking about. "Did you know they were going to die?"

"No. Nobody was supposed to die there. We were supposed to be reborn."

"You are going to explain what you mean, and you are going to stop talking like that. I am not one of your idiot friends."

"When you tell your Dad about us, what will he say?"

"He'll be fine with it. I've told you this."

"It's why you can't understand. Do you get that Dillon is the exception?
Most gay sons have to prepare themselves for coming out by accepting they
may lose their fathers forever. Even the ones who turn out to be wrong
had to be prepared to cut their parents out of their lives. You can't ever
understand what it's like to choose between lying to your parents about
who you are or losing them forever."

Eirinn doesn't say anything.

> "It's why homophobia is so much worse than racism. We may have
> the option to camouflage, but once we are out in the open we are
> totally alone, rejected by not just the outside world, but our families,
> our faith, and our friends. They were lost; they needed a family, and
> the ceremony was meant to cement their relationship as one. The rest
> was an accident."

Both lines of Seth's family trace straight back to Ireland within a few
generations. In fact every member of Following Shepard is white. At a
small, private school in rural Ohio, this is hardly surprising. JU's student
population is 88% white. Some of the individual colleges and graduate
programs go over 92%. Neither his perspective nor his frankness are
surprising to me. Attending JU has introduced me to a large population
of white people without academic qualifications who nonetheless consider
themselves experts on racism.

Being straight, much of the experience of the gay students I have been
following has been unknown or alien to me. Being Muslim, I have had
an outsider's perspective to their religious experience. But being third
generation Iranian, and frankly, visibly not white, has not come up until
right now.

I see Eirinn tense at the remarks, and intentionally not look at me; it's
a reaction I would easily recognize on anyone embarassed by a racially
insensitive friend. But I don't say anything. Now is not the time. And
deconstructing his point is too complicated to do here. But there are two
thoughts I will later coalesce:

Lumping together all experiences of racism, and for that matter, all experiences of homophobia, doesn't say anything useful about either. To then say that one is better or worse than the other is a useless conclusion.

In many situations, racism does isolate family members from each other. Immigrant families often split over the cultural disconnect caused by the assimilation of the younger generation into American culture.

They talk, for hours. Eirinn never raises his voice. The questions do not last long, before they are simply sharing memories and discussing life. The future, however, does not come up.

I spend the last hour of Seth's life with him, alone. Eirinn makes it to about 3 a.m., but he eventually falls asleep. Seth wakes again at 4, and we talk. He tells me about the path of Following Shepard, and where they stayed the last night. All told, he is alert for 45 minutes. When he falls asleep again, it is for the last time. At dawn, there is chaos in the room, but the crash cart makes no difference.

Seth McCam died at 6:35 a.m. At the entrance of the crash cart, Eirinn jolts awake and flattens to the wall in the corner of the room. When it leaves, the doctor looks, and says nothing. The nurses look, and as they leave, one comes close to a reassuring touch on his shoulder. Eirinn sees none of it. The moment the paddles go back in the cart, he crumples to the floor.

Tears and snot are streaming down Eirinn's face and he occasionally gasps for breath. We sit, still and in the corner of the room, for 20 minutes. He will not remember being walked to the car. I will remember every step. Eirinn leans heavily on me, but we do not stumble. The sun is fully over the horizon when we emerge from the front door of the hospital. Inside the car, we sit still again. The key is in the ignition, but the act of turning it seems too violent to complete. Every noise seems an act of cruelty.

27

We don't go in the attic until the 5th day. The dust is thick and undisturbed on every surface, but the boxes are in neat order, except for 4 boxes in the far corner from the entrance, the corners of which are worn and the sides of which are creased in several places. The room hasn't been entered in 6 months, but these boxes haven't been touched in 3 years. They're dated in Matthew McCam's hand.

Inside one box is a collection of items faded from being on display in the sunlight. At the top is a frame where there used to be parchment — two squares are saved from fading where something used to be taped. The discovery is on the back, a message also in Matthew's hand:

> On the occasion of your first communion
> When you receive the body of Christ you become one in the body with everyone who has ever received it. One with us, one with your whole family, ever. One with my father, before me.
> May God be with you today and always. Know that you are loved by your parents, your family, and even by your Grandpa who never met you but loves you still.
> Dad

Eirinn tells me that the frame hung in Seth's bedroom until Katelyn's death. According to Eirinn, a lot of things got broken then. It hasn't come

up before, and he barely finishes the sentence now. I don't press, only two
months after April.

I didn't get the answer in my brief time with Seth, but Eirinn did,
indirectly. Seth knew he was going to die. A lawyer contacted Eirinn in
mid-April — Seth's last will and testament had been arranged shortly after
their return from Ireland. Everything was given to Eirinn; the house, the
trust fund from his mother — everything Seth owned. I wasn't there when
Eirinn found out, but he did call me to help clean the house, which had
been unoccupied in the ensuing time.

I was there when we returned — we drove to the Gallagher home, and
the moment we stopped in the driveway Meara Gallagher rushed out. She
stopped short of the car when he hadn't opened the door yet, and wrung
her hands anxiously. Dillon came next, walking as though burdened. But
he arrived before Eirinn opened the door, and his arms were open for an
embrace. Meara put her hand on Eirinn's shoulder.

I got out of the car quietly, but when I shut the door, the noise reminded
them someone else was there. I was welcomed into the Gallagher home
without question, which surprised me given what we were about to discuss.
I built trust with Eirinn, and that was enough for the Gallaghers, as it had
been for Seth.

Eirinn choked out the story, and Dillon and Meara listened without
interrupting. By the end, Eirinn could barely speak. Meara sat next to him
and rubbed his back. They gave him tea, and Dillon walked with him to his
room. I was alone with Meara in the living room. She fidgeted, and cried.
Her expression was unreadable.

Meara had cried too when Eirinn went to college; Eirinn never understood
it. He was moving in with Seth, where he spent most of his time anyway,
and campus itself was only 20 minutes away. But when the car was packed,
and they were ready to drive, she stood at the doorway unable to speak.

The most difficult thing about being a mother, I expect, is also the central
theme. A mother's love is complete in a way that is difficult to grasp. She
had loved him before his birth. She had loved the screaming baby and the

ornery toddler as much as the adorable school child. There were times she could have done without the contrary preteen, but she loved every version of Eirinn as it came into existence. She never stopped, though, and that was the difficult part. At the end of the driveway was standing her son. But in the car with him was the end of the boy who used to hide behind her legs in public.

To love a child as they grow is to constantly experience love and loss. With each passing year, they are no longer the person they were, your feelings be damned (a sentiment they will get around to expressing sooner rather than later).

It's not a tragedy. It can't be reduced to what is sad, or happy. It comes in currents and tides, and at each moment it is moving in every direction. It is an infinite contradiction; a wellspring of both strength and weakness beyond comprehension or control. Standing in that living room, I finally understood the parents of the prodigal son. Rules, edicts, laws; they're just tiny things; paper and words.

Dillon spoke up.

"Thank you."

Amongst the many thoughts in my mind, 'I have no idea how to respond to that' bubbled to the surface. But I was far from speaking it aloud.

"You were there for my son on the worst day of his life. He'd never lost anyone close before. I'm not sure you know how much that means, that on the day he learned what loneliness really was, he wasn't alone."

"I think I do."

It's looked like surprise, but it was familiar disappointment on Dillon's face. "I'm sorry to hear that."

Under his gaze the week I'd been gone rested on my shoulders and I felt a need to be with my own father, and so I left.

The attic is hot today, and exceedingly cramped. After the third time I bang my elbow on the same cross beam, I get a splinter, curse and apologize, but I need to go downstairs. We do it together.

Eirinn gets out two thick, octagonal glasses and puts three ice cubes in each. And he tells me what his father told him the day after he returned home. He came down for breakfast the next morning, not knowing what else to do, and his father was waiting.

———————————————

"You never met my best friend."

On the Gallagher family trips to Ireland, Eirinn met every conceivable branch of family, and it seemed like everyone Dillon and Meara ever knew. But he had never met Aiden Connor. Connor was a schoolmate of Dillon's. They met when they were 8, and that morning, Dillon described them as inseperable. That is, until Connor died in paramilitary activity in the summer of 1979.

"It was the worst day of my life by a very wide margin. Aside from your Mother, Aiden was the closest friend I have ever had, and probably ever will. That was the day I learned what it is to have a hole in your life that it feels like you will never fill. I learned to grieve."

"We almost called you Aiden. I am very glad your mother talked me out of it. Eirinn, this is going to be bad. For a very long time. Today is going to be bad. And tomorrow might be worse. There's no roadmap out of the hole you're in."

"Are you trying to make me feel better?"

> "No. Not today. But I am here for you as you find your own way out. What I can tell you is what I learned from losing Aiden. Everyone who died that day — on both sides — believed they were saving the world for their families and friends. Whomever won — we knew it wasn't a world in which we could raise you. They loved their families. They loved their country and their faith. They loved with anger. They were wrong. Aiden saw love as a fire. He saw its passion and destruction and he named it fire. Love is tidal. It destroys, to be sure,

but only when you look at it through a magnifying glass. Love ebbs and flows over minutes and lifetimes. It is deep and alive and nations are shaped by its tremendous force. The world will always be saved by it. But sometimes, in the life of one man, it isn't enough."

www.ingramcontent.com/pod-product-compliance
Lightning Source LLC
Chambersburg PA
CBHW071409170626
46811CB00003B/1319